Benton met her gaze. "Is this the one, then?"

The one. Even though they were talking trees, not romance, her stomach felt hot. And not from the cocoa.

He was good with babies, thoughtful of grandmas, considerate of her being cold, godly and handsome. And that twinkle in his dark eyes?

It was almost enough to make her forget her no-pastor rule.

Almost. He was not for her. But whomever he married should count herself blessed.

"Yep." Her voice sounded a little tight. "You're the one. I mean, you found the one. It. The tree."

"All right then." Benton waved down one of the tree-lot employees. "Let's get it home."

Home. More than a house, but a place of love and laughter. For a moment, just a moment, she allowed herself to wish she were free to build a home, a family, with someone. With *the* one. Someone who might be a little like Benton.

But right now, a home and family were nothing but sugarplum dreams.

Susanne Dietze began writing love stories in high school, casting her friends in the starring roles. Today, she's an award-winning, RWA RITA® Award–nominated author who's seen her work on the ECPA and *Publishers Weekly* bestseller lists for inspirational fiction. Married to a pastor and the mom of two, Susanne lives in California and enjoys fancy-schmancy tea parties, the beach and curling up on the couch with a costume drama. To learn more, say hi or sign up for her newsletter, visit her website, www.susannedietze.com.

Books by Susanne Dietze

Love Inspired

Widow's Peak Creek

A Future for His Twins
Seeking Sanctuary
A Small-Town Christmas Challenge

Love Inspired Historical

The Reluctant Guardian
A Mother for His Family

Visit the Author Profile page at LoveInspired.com.

A Small-Town Christmas Challenge

Susanne Dietze

LOVE INSPIRED
INSPIRATIONAL ROMANCE

LOVE INSPIRED®

INSPIRATIONAL ROMANCE

ISBN-13: 978-1-335-75896-5

A Small-Town Christmas Challenge

Copyright © 2021 by Susanne Dietze

This edition published by arrangement with Harlequin Books S.A.

For questions and comments about the quality of this book, please contact us at CustomerService@Harlequin.com.

Love Inspired
22 Adelaide St. West, 40th Floor
Toronto, Ontario M5H 4E3, Canada
www.LoveInspired.com

Printed in U.S.A.

The Lord is my strength and song,
and is become my salvation.
—*Psalm* 118:14

For Mom and Dad, whose loving support and encouragement have meant the world to me. Thank you for always being there!
Merry Christmas!

Chapter One

The text message on Leah Dean's phone stopped her short.

"Hey, I see that smile." Irene Campos, Leah's boss on the skilled nursing ward at Creekside Retirement Villlage, looked up from the computer monitor at the nurses' station. "What's so funny? If it's a cat video, bring it over so I can watch, too."

"No video." Leah leaned against the counter, which had been decorated with an autumn leaf garland and a chalkboard sign that read Happy Fall, Y'all! "Rowena is summoning me."

"You make it sound like a demand."

"That's the word she used." Leah flipped her phone around so Irene could read the text. "She knows my shift is over, and she hereby summons me forthwith to her apartment, posthaste, before I return to my abode for the evening. Like we're in a medieval reenactment or something." She grinned. "I love her."

"Rowena's a character, all right."

A feisty ninety-year-old, Rowena Hughes lived in the apartments here at the retirement village. When she'd stayed in this ward last year to recover from heart surgery, she and Leah had grown close. "I wonder what she wants to talk about."

"Before you go, look what showed up on the counter." Irene stood up, her gaze landing on a familiar white box at Leah's elbow. "Chocolate-dipped macaroons from Angel Food Bakery. For you. No strings attached."

Now that was laugh-out-loud funny, so Leah let loose with a snort. Irene might be her boss, but she was also her closest friend. "You're bribing me with cookies, so I'll cover you on Thanksgiving, aren't you?"

"*Bribe* is such a strong word." She was the picture of innocence in cartoon-themed scrubs and a black cardigan the same shade as her bobbed hair. "But yes, guilty as charged. The whole family's gathering at my auntie's. I'll get to introduce everyone to Phil." Her new boyfriend.

"Sounds fun. Don't worry about me. I want to spend time with Grandma, and she's here anyway." *Here* being the retirement village complex, although in a different building than where Leah worked as a registered nurse, tending residents in need of intensive, short-term care. Other buildings housed apartments for active seniors, but Grandma's wing was for residents who required memory care.

Setting her phone on the counter, Leah reached for the hand sanitizer so they could dig into the cookies. Her phone vibrated, and Irene squinted at the screen. "Hold up, Leah. Does that say *Benton Hunt*?"

Leah read the follow-up text from Rowena. "Looks like she's summoned him, too. He's already on campus for a men's Bible study so she can talk to us at the same time. I'm pretty sure he's her pastor."

"He's not just *her* pastor. Or *a* pastor, honey. He's *the cute* pastor in town."

Cute-schmoot. "A person's looks don't matter when it comes to shepherding a flock."

"Well of course not, but come on, Leah. I may be dating Phil, but it's objectively factual that Benton Hunt is a total dreamboat. And his voice is like—so smooth. Like melted butter."

. Leah would concede he was attractive. Even more, he seemed like a genuine, nice guy during their brief interactions at Creekside Retirement Village, or CRV for short. She attended a different church in town, but he had a reputation as a good pastor. A good man.

But… "I'm not interested. Not in a hundred years."

"You haven't been on a date in a hundred years." Irene shut her eyes as if gravely disappointed.

Leah didn't want to talk about her dating life, or lack thereof. "Want a cookie?"

"Oh, no, they're yours."

Leah leveled Irene with a disbelieving look. Laughing, Irene popped the smallest cookie into her mouth. Then she made a soft *oh* sound.

"So good, right?" Leah bit into a soft cookie, allowing a moment for the chocolaty-coconut goodness to melt in her mouth. A few precious crumbs of coconut dusted the gray-topped counter like the first snowflakes that heralded a coming storm. Not that Leah had much experience with snow in Widow's Peak Creek. While it snowed plenty a short drive farther up into the Sierra Nevada Mountains, here in the foothills, snow would be something to get excited about. Just like these cookies. She'd finish them off after dinner.

But first, she had to drop by Rowena's apartment.

What was the purpose of this mysterious summons? "I'll see you tomorrow."

"Say hi to the dreamboat for me."

"Good night, Irene." Leah took her oversize purse from her locker, shoved the cookies inside and slung the cross-body strap over her head. Teasing though Irene had been, Leah's mood took a nosedive as she stepped out her building's automatic door into the early evening darkness. Why had Rowena asked to see her and a pastor simultaneously, right now? Was Rowena sick? While her heart surgery had been a success, Rowena had other medical concerns, such as high blood pressure and diabetes. What if something was wrong? Praying, Leah quickened her pace on the wide concrete path across the well-lit village campus.

The door to Rowena's apartment was ajar, so she took a step inside. "Rowena? It's Leah."

"Come in." Rowena perched on the couch, grinning like a child with a secret.

Leah strode straight to her friend's side and leaned in for a hug. "Is everything all right?"

"Don't I look all right?"

Leah leaned back, her nurse's gaze taking in Rowena's pallor, her eyes, her demeanor. All seemed normal. Better than normal, in fact. Rowena had donned sparkly clip-on earrings and a silky floral blouse. Her short, snow-white curls smelled of ammonia, like she'd visited the salon today for a fresh perm.

The apartment seemed normal, too, tidy and clean. Personalized touches accentuated the neutral decor in the two-room flat, from a sky blue afghan to crystal photo frames. If everything was hunky-dory, why the urgency?

Leah sat beside Rowena on the sofa. "You're lovely as ever, but your 'summons' had me worried for a second. What's up?"

"Rowena?" The masculine voice drew Leah's gaze around to the open door.

Benton Hunt paused in the threshold. Like Irene said, he was nice to look at, square-jawed, lean, his broad shoulders encased in a navy blue jacket over a white oxford shirt. A lock of cropped brown hair flopped onto his furrowed brow, and concern crinkled the skin around his dark eyes.

"Benton, forgive me for not getting up." Rowena gestured for him to take a seat in the chair adjacent to her. "You know Leah Dean?"

"We've met, yes."

Leah ignored the tiny voice of Irene in her head, noting the niceness of his smile. "Hello."

Rowena folded her hands on her lap. "You young people are busy, so I shall get straight to the point. Rather than wait until after my death for my possessions to be distributed, I have decided to dispense of my worldly goods while I am still alive."

Leah's jaw went slack. Rowena was a woman of considerable means, with a family legacy as old as the town itself. Her worldly goods were by no means unsubstantial. But why was Rowena telling Leah and Benton this? Perhaps, because Leah was her friend and he was her pastor, Rowena wanted to discuss her decision with them. While a lawyer or family member might be ideal for this sort of thing, Leah would gladly support Rowena however she could. "That's a lovely idea, Rowena."

"It is indeed." Benton's sharp gaze studied Rowena. "How can we help?"

Rowena pointed a bony forefinger at two legal-size manila envelopes on the coffee table. One bore Leah's name, and the other, Benton's. "Take those, for a start."

Understanding dawned, hot and humbling. Rowena had a gift for each of them. Such a kind gesture, one of many examples of Rowena's bighearted nature. But the thought of the day when Rowena was no longer in Leah's life pierced her like a spear of grief. She couldn't touch the envelope.

Benton didn't pick his up, either. "This is generous of you, Rowena, but—"

"Don't be such killjoys." Rowena's thin shoulders sagged in disappointment. "Humor me and open them."

Odd as it felt, Leah picked up the large envelope. It was thin and light in her hands, no heavier than a piece of paper. It must be a legal document informing her of the gift. Whatever it was Rowena wanted to leave to her—a book, a frame—would be treasured, because it came from her.

Leah was wrong. It was two sheets of paper, not one. The first was indeed a document, but it didn't look legal since it wasn't on letterhead, and the other was an eight-by-ten photograph. She looked at it, then the document, then the photo again.

Oh, no. This couldn't be right.

She dropped the pages like they were hot. "Rowena? There's been a mistake."

Benton didn't understand what he was looking at, either. Not that it wasn't spelled out in the document, but surely, this particular gift was meant to go to someone else. Leah was right. There'd been an error somewhere.

He glanced at Leah, her posture ramrod straight as she sat on the couch. She'd clearly just come off shift. Aside from the telltale giveaway of her dark red scrubs and ID tag clipped to a blue lanyard, she had a weary look about her, as if the day had been long and a trifle difficult. The delicate skin beneath her eyes showed the faintest of shadows, and a few tendrils of chestnut brown hair escaped her ponytail.

He had the utmost respect for nurses, but his estimation of Leah was greater than that. Although he didn't know her well, during their brief interactions she'd always struck him as a gentle person, whose easy smile and kind heart had earned her a reputation as an excellent, caring nurse here at Creekside Retirement Village.

He'd also noticed a few other things about her on those occasions, and she was probably unaware of the vertical crease that formed down her forehead when she concentrated. Or how she fiddled with the gold cross hanging from a delicate chain around her neck when she was concerned. She did both of those things now. Clearly, she was just as shocked by this gift of Rowena's as he was.

Rowena, however, clasped her hands beneath her chin and grinned, clearly enjoying their confusion. "No mistake. The photo says it all."

How was that possible? "This is your house, Rowena."

Known locally, if unofficially, as Hughes House, it had been Rowena's residence since her marriage to Hyland Hughes over sixty years ago. It had belonged to his family since a Hughes ancestor made a fortune selling tools and tinned foods to the miners who came to the area during the California gold rush in the 1850s. It wasn't the only grand home in town, but it was the last of its size that hadn't been turned into a bed-and-breakfast.

"My house, yes." Rowena's gray eyes sparked. "But now it's yours. Well, half of it is. The other half is for Leah. You each get half of my house."

In the next two seconds, a million thoughts raced across his brain, but he settled on one to speak aloud. "Thank you, Rowena, truly, but I can't accept. It's far too generous."

And far too expensive to keep up, even if he and Leah combined his pastor's salary with whatever she made as a nurse. Most of all, he didn't see how Rowena could expect him and Leah, two unmarried people who hardly knew one another, to live in it together. No matter how big the place was, there was no way.

Leah's gaze glanced off him before settling again on Rowena. "Yes, and it should stay in your family."

Rowena never had children, but her nephew lived in town. In fact, his wife, Judy, was the mayor of Widow's Peak Creek.

"My nephew Marty made it clear he and Judy don't want it. If they did, they'd already be living in it, but it's been sitting empty over five years now." Rowena threw her hands in the air. "No, all Marty and Judy want is the money they can get by selling it."

"I'm sure that's not true." Benton couldn't count the number of times folks had come to him for family counseling. Most of the time, family members miscommunicated but had the best of intentions. His family was an exception, of course. Not that he'd dwell on that now.

"Rest assured, Marty and Judy and their kids will get money from me, but the house is yours. Don't get me wrong, dears. I expect you to sell it, too, because it's not at all practical for either of you to live in. Sell it and split the proceeds. I know the money will be well used by you both. I only ask you ensure the new owner is worthy of it. I don't want it razed. It's in excellent shape despite its age and has a lot of life left in it." Rowena pointed at the page in his hands. "You must observe the other condition, of course."

"Condition?" Benton followed Rowena's pointing finger to the document in his hands. He scanned the words and caught on a single word.

Party.

In his earlier haste, he'd mistaken it to mean a legal party. "You want us to throw a party?"

"Oh, yes." Rowena practically crowed with delight. "I hosted it every year on December 21. Never was the house more glorious than at Christmastime." She sighed. "I can't do it myself anymore, and sometimes a person gets wistful, you know. Thinks of the past and wishes to experience something one more time."

Benton could understand thinking of the past and wishing for something. If he could go back to when he was fourteen and change what happened? Life would look a whole lot different.

Leah shifted on the couch. "I'm still not sure about this inheriting the house thing, Rowena, but I'm happy to help you throw a party. Do you have a list of friends to invite?"

"Of course not. The Gingerbread Gala is for everyone in town."

"The what." The way it came out of Leah, it didn't

sound like a question. Benton knew what it was, though. Not that he'd ever attended one, back in the day, but he'd first met Rowena the night of the Gingerbread Gala. Nineteen years ago.

Rowena flashed a quick glance at him before returning to smile at Leah. "The Gingerbread Gala is a fundraiser. In exchange for a reasonably priced ticket, back in the day, people came to our home for a festive, formal evening of singing carols, nibbling hors d'oeuvres, and making conversation, with a parting gift. A sweet little box of gingerbread people. It was always a rousing success. And don't fret, I'll pay for the catering and incidentals and such." She tapped her knee with one lipstick-red fingernail. "This year, I'd like the fundraiser proceeds to go to the town museum council headed by Faith Latham, who runs the antiques store. They're raising funds to purchase a site."

Benton rubbed his forehead, pressing against the suddenly forming ache. "I thought the mayor was opposed to a museum?"

"She is." Rowena couldn't hide a sly smile. "But the museum council is private. Mayors don't get to rule everything, do they?"

Benton swallowed down a groan. Maybe they didn't, but the mayor was Rowena's kin. A family disagreement *and* a party on December 21. Just over a month away, with live music, treats, gingerbread people and—did she say formal?

Much as he was in favor of a town museum, he was not the man for this.

Lord, You've given me a church to worry about. Not just the flock, but the facility, too. The roof's leaking, the refrigerator's on the fritz and the parish hall has to be ready by the Christmas Eve pageant or—

Rowena rapped his arm. "I've rendered you both speechless."

"This is a little shocking," Leah said with a forced smile. "I'm grateful, but I don't feel right about this."

"Neither do I." Benton could not accept a gift this large.

"I know, dears, which is exactly why you're the two perfect people to receive it. And I know you both can use the money. Go look at it right now. Those are your keys." She gestured to two white, business-size envelopes on the table. "We can talk about this more later, but for now, I must excuse myself. It's chicken cordon bleu night in the community dining room, and I don't wish to be late."

Thus excused, Benton stood. He'd never stand in the way of a hungry woman and a plate of cordon bleu. "Thank you, Rowena."

"Yes," Leah echoed. "Thank you."

Rowena gripped her bedazzled cane and stood. "You two sound like you inherited a Dumpster, but trust me. You're in for a treat."

They were in for something, all right. Benton wasn't at all comfortable with this, but he owed it to Rowena to at least go look at her house. His house. The one he now shared with a pretty nurse he hardly knew.

He gestured to the door. "Shall we, Leah?"

Chapter Two

Leah parked in front of Hughes House on Church Street, viewing the house through the fluorescent yellow glow of the streetlights. She'd passed the three-story house innumerable times, admired its redbrick, Greek Revival construction and grass-green shutters. It was a gem in Widow's Peak Creek's crown, but on this moonless, chill night, the dark edifice looked foreboding. She couldn't ignore the quiver in her stomach.

This place—this mansion, by town standards—was half hers? And the other half belonged to Benton Hunt? She'd better make sure Irene was sitting down tomorrow when she told her about this, because her friend was bound to swoon.

As soon as Benton parked his car behind hers and met her on the sidewalk, they started a slow pace up the circular drive to the house.

"My key's out already," she said when he pulled out his still-sealed white envelope. She'd ripped open her envelope the moment she parked her car. Within seconds they mounted the dark porch, the old wood beneath groaning under their shoes. She touched the key to the lock, expecting the latch to be stiff. To her surprise, the key turned easily. She paused before twisting the knob, though. "Did Rowena say anything about a burglar alarm on this place?"

"Not that I heard." He laughed, his teeth flashing in the dark. "We might be about to find out the hard way."

Irene was right about Benton having a nice voice. And he was nice to try to lighten the mood, so she joined in. "I'll be the one to get in trouble if the alarm goes off, seeing as how you're a pastor," Leah joked as she pushed open the front door. She took two steps inside, listening for a beep or chime to indicate a triggered alarm. All was silent, musty and dark, and she couldn't make out any pinpoints of red or green light to indicate an alarm panel. "No alarm, but this still feels weird and wrong."

"Maybe it'll be better once we turn on the lights. If we can find a light switch." Using the flashlight on his phone, Benton cast a bright beam of light over the cream-papered wall near the door. No switch. Skirting a circular marble table in the room's center, he walked around the perimeter of the room, but she stayed put. She wasn't usually afraid of the dark, but there was something creepy about being in a stale, creaky, abandoned house at night, unable to see anything except what was touched by his flashlight's beam. Maybe she should dig out her phone and lend a hand. Or, as the case may be, a light.

"Nothing." Ben frowned. "You'd think there'd be a switch by the door, but with old houses, you never know what you're going to get. Ah, here by the stairs."

He hurried toward a bronze plate at the bottom of a grand, curving staircase with a dark wood banister.

With a click, the foyer chandelier above them flickered to life, casting a glow on the black-and-white-tiled floor below.

"Better." Leah felt her shoulders relax. It was far, far less creepy now.

"Agreed. But still weird." Ben's smile was amused. "Kind of funny, because ten-year-old me would've eaten this up. Unlimited access to an old, abandoned house at night? I'd have spent hours looking for hidden passages, that sort of thing."

"Were you a fan of the Hardy Boys?"

"Maybe." His smile stretched to a grin. "Where should we start?"

"Wherever we can find a light switch. No more dark rooms."

He laughed. "Got it. First floor first?"

"Second floor second." She pointed to the room off to their right, keeping a wary eye for cobwebs and critters. "So, what exactly does Rowena want us to do right now? Get acquainted with the place before we plan a party, right? And then sell the house?"

"That's what I heard—unless you wanted to keep it. I guess I should've asked you that right away."

"No way could I buy you out. Besides, it's not practical for a single person to live here."

Blech. Spiderwebs formed an arch in the corner of the doorjamb. *Note to self: bring a long-handled broom when you clean this place out.* Ducking beneath the web far more than was necessary to avoid it brushing her hair, she followed Benton into the room.

He smiled over his shoulder at her. "Don't like spiders?"

"I don't even like hearing the word."

Laughing, he flicked on the switch, illuminating a red-and-pink floral-papered parlor furnished with sheet-covered mounds—couches, chairs and tables. He lifted a sheet halfway off a couch-shaped lump, sending a plume of chalky-smelling dust in the air. The couch beneath wasn't new by any means, but it reminded her of the comfortable sofa in Grandma's living room during Leah's growing-up years. "I love that color."

He eyed her similarly hued scrubs. "What is it called, anyway? Berry? Brick? Why are there so many names for one color?"

"They aren't one color at all." Her knuckles trailed the soft velvet, a deep-toned red that would blend well with everything from Christmas decor to modern cream pillows. "And I'd go with maroon. Berry is too pink, brick's too brown." Her grin let him know her color talk was playful, not snooty.

His lips twitched. "I'll come to you for advice next time I need to pick a paint swatch."

Yeah, right. As if they'd ever hang out once this house stuff was dealt with.

She peeked under a dusty cloth to reveal a mahogany tea cart, with delicate china cups and a matching pot still inside the glass case. For a split second, Leah imagined what it could be like to serve tea from that cart. Using good dishes like that would make a visit more formal, but at the same time, there would be something special about it. Like it was an investment in a relationship.

What a funny thought. She could hardly find time to sit down with a magazine and a mug of orange pekoe tea at her kitchen table.

Benton hitched his thumb at the door. "Want to see what else is down here?"

"Absolutely." The sooner they finished, the sooner they could lock this place back up and get some dinner. Leah's stomach clenched, reminding her that lunch hour was spent calming Grandma, and all she'd eaten since oatmeal at breakfast was that macaroon.

Moving counterclockwise around the house, they traveled through the parlor to a room void of contents except for a baby grand piano. From there they passed a family room that might've once been a library, judging by the shelves lining the walls, and entered a wide, airy area behind the foyer with French doors leading to the back porch and yard. Moving on past a utility room and a powder room, they moved into an outdated kitchen, complete with a breakfast nook and another door to the back porch. Leah grimaced at the chipped linoleum underfoot and vintage appliances. "Whoever buys this is going to want to do a major overhaul."

"You cook?" Benton's glance was admiring.

"I like to, but cooking for one gets old. I generally make up a batch of something and eat on it for a few days." Her panging stomach reminded her she'd finished the leftovers in the fridge, however. She'd have to make a sandwich tonight.

"I eat a lot of sandwiches. Is your schedule erratic, as a nurse?"

"Yours is much more so than mine." When his eyes narrowed in a questioning look, she shrugged. "My dad was a pastor, so I know the drill. On call 24-7."

"Ah. He's retired now?"

"No, he passed away some time ago." She walked through a butler's pantry to the dining room before he could offer condolences. Despite some stunning teal tiles set around the fireplace, she didn't stop but continued back into the foyer, where they'd started.

His lack of response told her he'd taken her hint about not wanting to talk about her dad, and she was grateful. Sometimes, if she started talking about her parents, she couldn't stop. Or she cried. She didn't want to do either of those things right now, and not with Benton.

On the second floor, the decor was more in keeping with the age of the house. Wallpaper, heavy furnishings, fireplaces and cozy chairs in the four bedrooms gave off a decidedly Victorian vibe. In the largest bedroom, the overhead lightbulbs flickered, failing as if ready for the bulbs to be changed, but the effect was like candlelight. It was easy to imagine how this must have looked in an earlier day. Welcoming, warm and homey.

She pushed back the heavy drape and peered down onto the circular drive. "This house makes me think of a Dickens-era Christmas. I almost expect to see a horse and carriage outside."

"Jingle bells and carols? I agree."

The same strange yearning she'd experienced when she examined the tea cart downstairs swelled within her chest. She wasn't a huge history buff, but she couldn't help entertaining certain ideas in a house like this. Maybe not a real carriage ride, but other, still-attainable Dickens Christmas-type thoughts, like children playing and visitors coming in from the cold. Like the joy of living with a family again.

Like maybe she wasn't as at peace with the idea of being single as she thought she was.

He whistled, drawing her attention to the sampler hanging on the wall. "Look at this."

Grateful for the distraction from her thoughts, Leah came to look at it. "'The Lord is my strength and my song,'" she read. "I like that verse. Beautiful needlework, too. Looks old."

"My mom had a sampler with that verse on it. Not quite as fancy." His sipping-chocolate eyes were warm, gazing at her, and her stomach lurched in a way that had nothing to do with her need for a square meal.

Great, so now she was yet one more of the Widow's Peak Creek females who considered Pastor Benton Hunt attractive personally, not just objectively. Not that it meant anything or ever would. She was not interested in romance. And with him of all people.

"I don't have time for this."

She didn't think she said it aloud, but his gaze sharpened. Then he lowered the Bible. "I'm glad you said something, Leah, because to be honest, I don't have the time, either. We don't know one another all that well, but I'd like it if we agree to speak our minds with each other."

A rational suggestion, and one that would save them time. "Sounds good."

"Then here's what I'm thinking. You and I both—"

"Who's here?" A feminine shout from downstairs startled Leah out of her skin. "I'm two seconds away from calling 911. Show yourselves now."

The sharp-edged voice held a familiar cadence. "Is that the mayor?"

"I think so." Benton blinked like he'd been startled, too. "We'd better make ourselves known."

Leah had no memory of gripping the front of Ben's jacket in her fright, but her hands were tangled there when she looked down. Her hands fell at once. "Sorry."

"No worries." He led the way out. "Mayor Hughes,

is that you? It's me, Benton Hunt from Good Shepherd Church, with Leah Dean from Creekside Retirement Village."

Leah had never met the mayor in person, but there was no mistaking the woman in the lime-green trench coat glaring up at them from the foyer. A middle-aged woman with cropped platinum hair and a penchant for expensive clothes, Judy Hughes stood out in town. Her eyes narrowed as she stared at them. "A pastor and, what are you, a nurse? Taking advantage of Rowena's absence to rob her blind, is that it?"

Leah didn't appreciate the mayor's insinuation, but this was all a misunderstanding. "Perhaps we should start over. I cared for Rowena after her heart surgery last year, and Benton is her pastor. Tonight, she gave us keys and asked us to come by—"

"Pretty common story, isn't it? 'Caregivers' taking advantage of vulnerable seniors." The mayor's long, hot pink nails rapped the plastic of her cell phone case. "You criminals picked the wrong mark."

Leah's vision narrowed. "Surely you didn't call us criminals?"

"You heard me."

Enough was enough. Leah stomped past Benton down the stairs. "Go ahead and call the police. We have nothing to hide, Madam Mayor, and I resent your insistence that *Pastor* Hunt and I have ill intentions."

If her tone was sharp, so be it. The mayor had crossed a line, and Leah would not stay silent in the face of bullies wielding insults. Not anymore.

Criminal.

It wasn't the first time Benton had been called that

word. But as much as he appreciated Leah's defense—her heavy emphasis on his title of pastor didn't escape his notice—it would be better for all of them if he and Leah could turn the other cheek and calm down a potentially volatile situation.

"If we intended to rob or damage Rowena's property, we wouldn't have turned on every light in the house, broadcasting our presence here. I suspect that's how you knew someone was in the house." Thankfully, he'd tucked Rowena's document in his jacket pocket earlier. At the time, he didn't know why he felt led to do it, but now he suspected it was God's nudge. "If I may approach you, this paper might explain things."

"Fine."

He hurried down the stairs, holding out the paper.

She snatched it from his hand, holding it at a distance so she could focus. Then she gasped. "This is preposterous. She can't give you this house."

"I don't know anything about the legalities, Mrs. Hughes. All Leah and I know is what Rowena said tonight, and she asked us to look at the house. May I have the paper back, please?"

Reluctantly, she returned it. "We'll see about this. Now, I suggest you two leave."

Leah's arms crossed over her chest. "Actually, I think *you* should."

The mayor flinched as if slapped. "How dare you? This is my aunt's home."

"I'm sure what Leah meant was, she and I are in possession of the keys. We can't leave before you do, so we can lock up." Benton fought hard to keep his tone diplomatic. "If you'll allow us a moment to turn off the lights?"

"Not without me keeping an eye on you two," the mayor insisted. "And first thing tomorrow, I'll be calling my lawyer."

After an awkward few minutes of turning off lights and locking up the house under the mayor's suspicious eye, Benton walked with Leah down the circular drive toward their cars. "It might not be a bad idea for us to talk further. Are you up for a quick bite at Del's Café?"

"I'm pretty hungry. And I could definitely use some comfort food about now."

Hughes House wasn't far from the town's historic Main Street, where Del's was located, and within fifteen minutes they were seated across from one another in a booth, orders placed, ice water in his hand and a mug of chamomile tea in hers. Neither had required a menu to order.

"You like chicken potpie, too?" It was Benton's top choice at Del's on cool nights like this.

"My favorite thing at Del's. High calorie, for sure, but who cares tonight? It's not every day you and I get called criminals." Leah shuddered. "You did an excellent job of defusing the situation, though. I've got too hot a temper, as you could tell."

"I can get pretty angry when the situation warrants it, I assure you."

"You're a pastor, though. You're good at calming people."

Of course he wanted to live a life of peace, giving others the benefit of the doubt, looking for amicable solutions, but not just because he was a pastor and a man of faith. In truth, he had a lifetime of experience soothing unstable situations. Growing up as the child and brother of alcoholics, he learned at an early age how to cool flaring tempers. Fast.

Not that he wanted to think about his dad or his brother right now. He sipped his water, ordering his thoughts. "It's difficult to wrap my head around everything that happened tonight, but it looks like we have two different issues to deal with. One is the house. I feel incredibly uncomfortable about the whole thing. A house is too big a gift."

"I feel the same. I love Rowena, but it's not like I'm her niece or something. People will probably agree with the mayor and think we're taking advantage of her."

His glance was sympathetic. "I don't know you well, but I'm pretty sure you haven't had any ulterior motives in your friendship with Rowena."

"I'm sure you haven't, either. Her financial situation has honestly never crossed my mind."

"We know it, and the Lord knows it. I guess we have to let others' opinions go." Easier said than done, but he had to remind himself daily of this truth. "Speaking of opinions, though, we may want to seek a legal one."

"That paperwork wasn't official. I'll ask Rowena if we may consult her lawyer for details, and then we'll get a clearer picture of what's going on." She swallowed her tea. "You said the house is the first issue. What's the second issue?"

Their potpies arrived, golden-crusted and hot. After they thanked their server and Benton said grace, they broke open the flaky crusts with their forks, releasing fragrant steam. Benton glanced at her while he sprinkled pepper over the top. "The second issue is the Gingerbread Hoedown or whatever."

"Hoedown?" Leah's full lips twitched with mirth. "It's a gala. Not the same thing at all."

"Maybe not, but hoedowns are fun."

"You attend them regularly, then?"

"I'm a pastor. I'm sure your dad attended pretty much every kind of event his parishioners invited him to, as well. I went to my first baby shower not that long ago. Now I guess I get to add gala to the list." He took a bite of tender chicken.

"Well, it'll be my first gala, too. Although I can't say I'm excited."

Oh, yeah, she'd said she didn't have time for everything in front of them. "You mentioned your schedule is pretty booked?"

"Not with anything official, besides work. My grandma lives at CRV, though, and I spend a lot of time with her. I've never thrown a formal party before. It sounds…daunting."

Her hazel gaze implored him. Paralyzed him. So lovely, those eyes—

Snapping back to attention, he returned his attention to his dinner. "I've never thrown a formal party, either, but I'm pretty sure these things are usually planned months in advance."

"That's what I was thinking. We're behind schedule before we start. I'm sure you're swamped at church, too, with Christmas coming. I imagine you have a choir concert and a pageant, for starters."

"Yes, to both. The pageant is Christmas Eve. It's been held in the parish hall for fifty years, but we discovered some wood rot in the stage steps and the linoleum is shabby. Possibly even dangerous if someone trips on a loose corner. I'm making repairs as fast as I can, so we can keep the tradition alive."

"Yikes. Not by yourself, I hope."

Precisely by himself, as a money-saving measure. He'd been urged to do so by a parishioner—Odell Donalson was the most budget-conscious man Benton had ever met—but Benton agreed to undertake the repairs. He'd thought the projects might be a fun change of pace. He had nothing better to do in his evenings, anyway. "The church budget is tight. I can handle it, though. Anyway, despite how busy the next few weeks will be, and regardless of the legalities of giving us the house, Rowena is a special person. I don't know how to throw a gala, but I'll do it for her. I'm not saying you should do it, though."

"No, I'm in, too. Rowena is one of a kind." Leah poked a carrot with her fork.

They finished their supper, conversing easily on a wide range of light topics—her attendance at one of the other churches in town, their favorite treats at Angel Food Bakery and a funny account of her helping a patient find a misplaced television remote this afternoon. "It was beneath his pillow the entire time," she said, as she forked up her last bite of potpie.

"How many times did you ask him if it was there? Twice?"

"Yes, and after I got down on hands and knees to look under the bed." She laughed. "Nursing isn't always about medicine."

"It's about compassion, which you seem to show a lot of."

She shook her head, but a faint flush turned her cheeks pink. Leah was as thoughtful a woman as she was lovely. Maybe, if he were able to consider dating, she'd be the sort of person he'd like to get to know.

But then she'd find out what a mess his family was. Full of pain and secrets. And they weren't believers. He'd been completely ineffective helping them toward salvation or healing. What sort of pastor did that make him?

A sorry one.

But he tried to be a decent man, nevertheless. He took the check before she could. "My treat."

"Thanks. I hope you have a restful night ahead. Or are you working in the parish hall?"

"I'd planned on it, but the day took an unexpected turn. Are you heading home?"

"Oh, yes." She gathered her purse. "I need to get back to Ralph."

Wait, she was married? "Ralph?"

Her face took on a dreamy, loving look. "My mini schnauzer. I love him to bits."

Why did he feel so relieved at finding out Ralph was a dog? *Knock it off, Benton.* They were teamed up for an unusual Christmas, thanks to Rowena, but after that? They'd go back to nodding at one another on the street, and it would be for the best.

But until then, they had a lot of work to do. Together.

"We should exchange numbers." He handed her his cell phone. She did the same, and when he handed hers back over the table, the faint flush to her cheeks had bloomed into a full-fledged blush, as red as the cracked leather seat she sat on.

They were being watched, and his gaze rose. Then he grinned at the couple who'd just entered the café, staring at him and Leah.

"Hey, Kellan, Paige. Where's Poppy?" The bookstore manager and preschool teacher weren't just his parishioners, but his dear friends, too. Their baby girl was only a few weeks old, but here they were, without her.

"My mom insisted on taking Poppy so we can have a dinner date. I don't want to be gone more than an hour or so, though. I miss her already." Paige looped her arm through her husband's. "Hi... Leah, is it? I've seen you in Kellan's bookstore before."

"Yes. Hi." Boy, did Leah look uncomfortable under his friends' smiling scrutiny. "Nice to see you both. I'd, um, better get going, but I'll be in touch, Benton. Thanks for dinner." Leah hardly glanced at him as she scooted out of the booth, squeezing past Kellan and Paige.

The moment she was gone, Paige gripped Benton's forearm. "We wrecked your date. I am so sorry."

"Not a date."

"Even worse, we interrupted a ministry meeting?" Paige looked stricken.

"Nothing like that. I'll fill you in later. Have a nice dinner, you two. Talk to you soon?" He rose and clapped Kellan on the shoulder. Kellan knew Benton had no intention of dating anyone, despite attempts other parishioners made to pair him with their nieces, daughters and friends.

"Yeah, sure." Kellan waved.

Outside, the cool night air snaked beneath his jacket collar. He dug out his car keys, debating between calling it a day or spending on hour on the parish hall stage. First, though, he checked his cell phone. Two texts had come in while he was paying the bill.

The first was, unsurprisingly, Odell Donalson, requesting a status update on the parish hall.

The second text was from Dad.

Son, you're not going to believe this...

Oh, Benton believed it all right. What sort of far-fetched circumstances had befallen Dad now? Regardless, they'd require a sum of money to set right. Money that Benton, and his father, both knew wouldn't really be going toward everyday expenses, since he'd been unemployed for a while now. No, Dad would use it to pay off a gambling debt. Or maybe he was drinking again. He said he hadn't had a drink in six months, but Benton never quite believed him.

Sighing, Benton looked up at the dark, moonless night, searching for clarity among the stars. *How do I honor my father, God? I want to do the right thing. Your will.*

He'd made so many mistakes before, in the name of helping his family and protecting their reputations. Mayor Hughes hadn't called him a criminal for nothing.

But things had changed since then, and nowadays, he wouldn't take another step without God. He prayed as he walked to his car, listening for an answer, but tonight, all he heard was the autumn breeze rustling through the trees.

It's all right, Lord. I'll wait. As long as it takes.

Chapter Three

The next afternoon, Irene sidled alongside Leah's chair at the nurses' station. "Isn't it time for you to go to that appointment with Rowena's lawyer?"

Leah glanced at the time in the lower right corner of the computer screen. "Just about, but Mrs. Consuelos is complaining of pain. I'm sending a note to the doctor."

"I can handle it while you freshen your makeup."

Irene was as subtle as a sledgehammer. "For the lawyer?"

"Of course not." Irene groaned in exasperation. "For the cute pastor."

Benton Hunt.

Earlier today, Leah had told Irene everything that happened last night, from Rowena's gift to the potpie. She even mentioned how well Benton had calmed down the mayor. His tone had been like a father's to a child, almost tender as he'd explained things. He didn't get defensive or raise his voice, despite the mayor's abrasive manner.

He was a good pastor. A good person. His character

was even more attractive than his handsome face. No way would she tell Irene that part, though.

Last night, she'd called Rowena after feeding Ralph. Rowena crowed with laughter at hearing Mayor Hughes was put out. She was also agreeable to Leah and Benton speaking to her lawyer, so Leah called the law office in the morning to schedule an appointment. The lawyer had an opening that day, and fortunately, Benton's schedule was free at the appointed hour.

Irene's huff drew her back to the present. "If you don't hurry, you won't have time to change clothes, much less reapply your blush."

"What's wrong with this?" She looked down at her autumn-leaf-patterned scrubs. She was a nurse. Everything she did after work, she did in scrubs. Besides, she looked festive, since it was days before Thanksgiving.

"Really?" Irene's disappointed voice rose two octaves.

Leah hit Send on the email and rose to grab her purse. "I'll swipe on lip gloss, okay?"

"Whatever. Text me later. I want to know everything."

"I'm sure it'll be boring stuff in legalese." She knew well that wasn't what Irene meant, of course. Her friend would want to know about Benton, but the truth was, there would never be anything between them beyond friendship. Irene knew better than to think Leah would ever date—

"Benton?" She drew up short as he strode up the concrete walkway toward her, hands stuffed in the pockets of his blue jacket. "What are you doing here?"

His smile made his eyes crinkle. "I was visiting a parishioner and thought, since I'm here, maybe we could carpool. Parking can get tight in the business district."

"How thoughtful. Sure." Irene would break into applause once she found out they were carpooling, if she wasn't already spying on them from the glass door.

The buildings on campus were connected by wide walkways leading to the central hub of the lobby, the only way in or out of the facility, except for emergency exits. Benton opened the lobby door for her. "I like your scrubs. Nice and seasonal."

Take that, Irene. "Thanks. The patients seem to enjoy it when we wear fun scrubs. It's a good conversation starter."

"Like right now, for example. Launching us to the obvious question, what are you doing for Thanksgiving?"

"Working." They traversed the lobby and once outside, he indicated his car, a serviceable gray sedan parked close by. Very pastor-like, unshowy and fuel efficient. He unlocked it with his fob and opened her door for her. Opening the lobby doors for her was one thing, but a man hadn't opened a car door for her in… So long ago she'd forgotten.

Once she slid into the clean car, he hurried around the hood and slipped behind the wheel. "Does that happen a lot? Working on holidays?"

"It depends, but I don't mind. I wasn't going to see my brothers for Thanksgiving, anyway. We grew up in Pinehurst, not too far from here, but they're both in the Bay Area now. I'd moved there, too, before Grandma— well, she's a lifelong resident of Widow's Peak Creek, and I took a job at CRV so I could be close to her. What about you? Will you be with your family?"

"Not for Thanksgiving. I'll be with Kellan and Paige, who we ran into last night. As for Christmas, though, I'm not sure. I grew up here, but my family moved away before I finished high school. I came back about five years ago to be the pastor of Good Shepherd." He pulled the car onto the road skirting the creek that gave the town its name. Today, the water was dull gray, reflecting the leaden sky above. The air coming through the vents smelled damp, like rain was coming.

He turned on the heater, and it felt good on her cold feet. "I'm glad Rowena's lawyer could fit us in this afternoon. Once we have some answers on whether this whole gift thing of hers is legal or not, we can move forward."

"It was hard to sleep last night, thinking about it." Benton turned up historic Main Street, which would take them to the north end of town. "This is such a weird situation. I mean she's essentially giving us a good sum of money, and she said something about knowing it would be well spent. I never had a conversation like that with her, though." His eyes widened and he glanced at her. "Sorry. That sounds like I'm fishing for your personal information, but I was just thinking aloud. Honest."

Honest. Something they'd agreed to be with each other, so she might as well be up-front. "Actually, I did tell Rowena I'm saving up for something. I never thought she'd view our conversations as my asking for money, though. I feel awful now."

His glance took in her hands, fumbling with her purse strap—she always fidgeted when she was nervous. "I'm sure she didn't take it that way. I doubt she'd give you half her house if she disapproved of your intentions for the proceeds."

True. "Still, everything about this situation is awkward."

"No argument from me. But I think God is more than capable of working with awkward beginnings."

"You're right. Good will come out of this." It had to, for Grandma's sake.

He pulled onto the main street of the business district. As he'd said, there weren't any parking spaces to be found in front of the office of Rowena's lawyer. "I'm going to have to park around the corner. Do you mind a short walk? It might rain, so I'm happy to drive in a circle in case a closer spot opens up."

"Nah, I've got a hood on my jacket."

Halfway up the block, he found a snug spot and parallel parked. She let herself out of the car as a chill gust of wind hit her square in the face. He joined her on the cracked sidewalk. "For what it's worth, I know how I'll use the money. There's so much delayed maintenance that needs to be done at Good Shepherd. A roof is the most expensive, but the kitchen could use new pipes and commercial grade appliances. Maybe this is God's way of providing for those needs."

How generous. And surprising. After all, pastors had their own financial needs. She'd half expected him to put his share of the money toward something sensible. But to spend all of it on a roof and appliances?

"That's generous of you, Benton."

"Hardly. I'm completely selfish when I say these fixes will free up my time to do other things. I'm up late each night making repairs to the parish hall before the pageant, remember?" He shoved his hands in his jacket pockets as they rounded the corner. "Besides, it's better if I don't have a lot of money at my disposal. Might as well spend this on something that can ease the burdens of my parishioners so we're freer to bless the people of Widow's Peak Creek. I get excited thinking about the things we can do once we're in better repair. Vacation Bible school, after-school programs, community programs. What about you? Did you tell Rowena you're saving up for a vacation?"

Leah blinked. *Better if he didn't have money at his disposal?* What did that mean?

None of your business, Leah. But he'd told her his plans, so she might as well tell him hers. "Much as I've always wanted to lie on a beach in Hawaii, no exotic vacations for me. My grandma Clare has stage six Alzheimer's, and if you've been inside CRV's Memory Care Unit, you know it's nurturing, clean, safe. But it's small. Limited. She wants more mobility but there's not a fenced, designated space at CRV for memory care patients to have that. However, there's a great facility on the Coast with specialized staff and activities, where she'd have the space to walk around outside. Insurance won't cover all of it, so I've been saving to make up the difference."

Their pace slowed as they neared the law office. Instead of taking the last few steps, he looked down at her, his lips turned up in a smile that looked downright astonished. "And you called me sacrificial, wanting a fixed roof?"

"She sacrificed for me." She couldn't meet his gaze anymore. Talking about Grandma Clare, well—it made her emotional. Just saying the word *Alzheimer's* gave her a painful lump in the throat. "She gave up a lot for me, so I'm not going to abandon her now."

"Of course not. You're a good granddaughter, Leah, and the Coast isn't that far. I'm sure you'll see plenty of her."

"Daily, I hope. That's part of what I've been saving for. The cost of living is higher in the city, so I'll need more money if I'm going with her. Even though she doesn't recognize me—well, it doesn't matter. She and I are leaving Widow's Peak Creek together."

Benton's gut twisted in sympathy for Leah. She'd been walking a rough road, caring for a family member with Alzheimer's. He hadn't experienced it himself, but the disease had affected a few parishioners. He also knew firsthand the helpless ache of loving someone who suffered, and that helplessness rose in his chest now. How could it not, when he thought of his father and his brother? "I'm sorry, Leah. For you and for your grandma."

He was also sorry she'd be leaving town. She had a life here, friends and a church, and separating from those relationships was never easy. There was something else tingeing his regret, though. Something akin to disappointment that they wouldn't have time to become better friends. Which was ridiculous, considering friendships with attractive females were not something he should be thinking about at all—

"Pastor Benton?" An older woman with wispy hair dyed the color of canned peaches marched toward them, her narrow gaze fixed with unabashed curiosity on Leah. "Fancy running into you here. What are you doing away from Good Shepherd?"

As if he needed a reminder why he couldn't form friendships with single women, here was Exhibit A. "Hi, Maude. Just running an errand."

If she wanted more of an explanation, he hated to disappoint her, but it wouldn't be prudent or considerate to discuss the private circumstances of Rowena's will. Especially before he and Leah spoke to the lawyer.

Maude grabbed his elbow in a viselike grip that threatened to cut off circulation to his hand. "Guess who I just saw. Clementine Simon. She's visiting the accountant across the street."

"That's nice. I hope everything is well." It sounded harsh, maybe, but Benton recognized the gleam in Maude's eye. Since a few older ladies at church had taken credit for making a match of Kellan and Paige, Maude had seemed inclined to get in on the fun. She'd brought various single women from church to his attention, her attempts as unsubtle as they were unwelcome. Catching on, he'd informed Maude he was not interested in marrying anyone. It was best that he put a stop to Maude's thinking now before she took things with Clementine any further.

Maude released his arm, sniffing. "Clemmie needs support, that's all. I pray every day that God sends a husband to help her."

"If that's His will, nothing can stop it. By the way, this is Leah Dean. Leah, Maude Donalson."

"Hello," Leah said.

"You don't go to our church."

Benton's jaw fell. That was not the welcoming message he hoped his parishioners spread when meeting folks.

Leah's smile was gracious, though. "I attend Creekside Community."

"I'm afraid Leah and I have an appointment, but I'll see you Sunday." He smiled at Leah, gesturing toward the door to the law offices. "Shall we?"

"Nice to meet you, Maude." Leah reached for the door.

"Hmph." Maude pursed her lips.

Benton followed Leah into the well-appointed lobby. Once the door shut behind them, he sighed. "Sorry about that."

"She's teasing you for dating Clementine Simon, huh? I know her a little bit. She's great."

"No way. I mean, Clementine is a great person, but she's my parishioner. I'm not dating her, never will." Since the death of her sister made her guardian of her young niece and nephew almost two years ago, she'd come to Benton on and off for spiritual counsel. It wouldn't be appropriate for him to pursue her even if he'd wanted to—which he didn't. For her part, Clementine nursed a broken heart over someone from her past. "Maude means well, but I don't appreciate what she did today."

"Parishioners are interested in their pastors' lives. My dad was a pastor, remember? I know what it's like to live in a fishbowl, with everyone watching what we did." Her smile slipped, and something almost caustic tinged her tone.

"Not just pastors', I don't think. Widow's Peak Creek is a small town. People talk, but we can't control what others do. Just what we do, and we haven't done anything wrong."

If he could control what others did, his dad and his brother, Jarod, would be saved and established in their recoveries. They'd call to say they loved him, not to ask for money.

"May I help you?" A blonde receptionist gazed up at them.

Thankfully, Leah was on the spot, informing the young woman of their appointment. Within a few seconds, they were ushered into the lawyer's office, and in under ten minutes they were out again to a world dampened by a thick drizzle. They didn't talk much while they hurried down the sidewalk back to the car. Once they were seated and he had the car's heater going, Leah lowered her jacket hood. "I guess that settles that. Rowena's of sound mind, the gift is legal and we're throwing a party."

"A big, fancy schmoozefest." Benton couldn't help but want to lighten the mood as well as ease the concerned line between her eyebrows. "I'm guessing we can't cater pizza for this shindig, then?"

She laughed, as he'd hoped. "Maybe we should serve hot wings. From henceforth it'll be known as the Hot Wings Gala."

"Hot Wings *Hoedown*, you mean."

"Alas, gingerbread seems to be the name of the game here. And *fancy*. Does that mean we have to serve caviar or something? I don't even know what it tastes like."

"I do, and I'm putting my foot down on that one. No fish eggs." He stifled a shudder as he pulled into traffic.

"That bad?"

"Maybe it was the batch I had? I'm sure a caterer will have quality stuff."

She snapped her fingers. "I totally forgot we could hire a caterer. That'll make this so much easier. Do you know any good ones?"

"A few. Perk of being a pastor I guess. I know people."

"We'd better make up a to-do list." She dug into her purse and pulled out a notebook. "Ca-ter-ers." She said it slowly, as she wrote down the word. "What else do we need?"

He racked his brains to remember. "Music? Singing?"

"She did mention carols. I forgot. We're going to need to decorate the house, too. When I spoke to Rowena this morning, she said there are decorations in the attic, but I suspect we'll want, or need, to buy some things. I have no idea when I'll get it done."

"Not just you, okay? I'm helping. This is a team effort."

He could feel her smile before he turned his head to meet her gaze. "Thanks, Benton."

They brainstormed the rest of the way to the CRV staff parking lot, where he parked next to the small red SUV he recognized as hers from last night. As she jotted *Christmas tree(s)* on her list, he turned off the ignition. "Think of at least one thing you want the caterer to include for you, okay? So there's something on the menu just for you."

"Stuffed mushrooms." She didn't even have to think, which made him happy. "You? What do you want your treat to be?"

"Anything with bacon."

"Deal." She wrote *mushrooms* and *bacon* on the list. Then, sighing, she tapped the list with the point of her pen. "This whole gala thing won't be easy, but I'll do it for Rowena. And for Grandma Clare. And for your church repairs."

"I just hope those repairs get completed before my family finds out there's money coming my way."

He'd said that aloud? *Great.*

He did what he always did when he stepped in a mud puddle of his own making and offered an apologetic smile. "Sorry. That just tumbled out. Not exactly the sort of thing to say to an acquaintance."

"We might not know one another well, but everyone has problems. Even pastors."

She was kind, but regret gnawed at his stomach. He shouldn't elaborate, but he'd blurted that bit about not wanting money on hand, so he felt he should explain somehow. "My dad and brother are alcoholics. I don't broadcast it, but Jarod, my brother, is in recovery, holding down a job in Tahoe, doing great. My dad says he's not drinking, but he isn't working. He might be gambling—I'm not sure. He lives in the county, but we don't see each other much. Our relationship is based on him reaching out when he needs something. Like rent money that never quite ends up with the landlord, if you know what I mean."

"I do." Her eyes softened. "I'm sorry."

"It's caused some issues, for sure." Like what happened when he was fourteen years old.

He only shared it with a select few, although several other folks in town had long memories. Like Mayor Hughes, who'd been quick to remind him of his past when she caught them at Hughes House and called them *criminals.* But even she didn't know the whole story.

A splat hit the windshield, dragging him from his reverie. In those few seconds that he'd been lost in thought, the drizzle had given way to heavy raindrops, which now became a full-fledged downpour. She watched him instead of the rain-battered windshield, though, with that concerned line dissecting her brows.

"Addiction is tragic." Her voice was kind. "I don't mean to pry, but how is your mom doing with it?"

"She passed when I was two. Cancer."

Leah looked at her fingers. "I'm sorry. I mentioned that my dad died, but I lost my mom the same night. Car accident. I was in middle school. No matter what age you are, it's rough. Grandma Clare raised me and my brothers from that point onward. She was there when I needed her, and now that she's the one in need, I'm going to be there for her. Even though my brothers think I'm wasting my time because she doesn't recognize me most of the time."

Benton didn't miss her shifting the conversation off her parents. "It's not a waste of time. It's called love."

"I admit, it doesn't feel like love sometimes. Lately when she does remember me, she gets agitated, and it's hard." She'd gone so quiet, it was difficult to hear her over the rain pounding against the car roof and windshield. "Trust me, I'd much rather her be at peace than know who I am."

"That's remarkable, Leah. Your choice to love even in tough times is a beautiful thing."

"You're a good pastor, saying that. After I dumped a lot of heavy stuff on you, too."

"That's not a pastoral thing, that's a human thing. I don't share what I hear, either. Besides, you listened to me talk about my family. I tend not to talk about them much, but sometimes we gotta let off steam."

"Yeah, we do. I won't say anything, either. Thanks for listening to me. It does help to verbalize things once in a while." Her eyes brightened with moisture as she gathered her oversize purse. "I should get home. Thanks for the ride. Should we meet up again after Thanksgiving? Maybe at Hughes House, to figure out how we'll do the Gingerbread Gala?"

They set up plans, and Benton waited until she'd driven away before grabbing a hamburger for a hasty dinner at church while he worked on the parish hall. There was plenty to do to make it presentable for the pageant on Christmas Eve. Thankfully, the other maintenance needs could wait until after the Gingerbread Gala and the sale of Hughes House.

How long will the sale take, Lord? Please find us a buyer quickly, so Leah can get her grandma settled sooner than later. Benton prayed with hammer in hand, two nails in his lips, nailing a fresh step in place at the stage. *In the meantime, Lord, what about this gala? You know neither of us knows what we're doing. I trust You to give us what we need.*

Benton could do nothing more but wait for God's guidance while he saw to the tasks at hand. Aside from the pageant, there was the canned food drive, a gift collection for needy kids, the choir concert and about a hundred other things relating to the season.

He should be thinking about them as he sanded a rough spot on the stairs. Instead, he thought about Leah—and not in any way related to the gala. He couldn't ignore the way she talked about her grandma. How pretty her smile was. How much he enjoyed her sense of humor.

Disgusted with himself, he tossed down the sandpaper. He needed to stop thinking about Leah. He had to get his family in order before he was worthy of bringing a woman into his life. And even if his family turned around tomorrow, what did it matter? Leah was leaving Widow's Peak Creek.

It was for the best that he put a stop to his thoughts and focus on the task at hand. He had a life plan and he needed to stick to it. No romance. No marriage. No family until Dad and Jarod were in a good place.

In the meantime, he'd keep praying, keep working, do what he had to do to give Rowena the Gingerbread Gala of her dreams. Leah would move away, and then he wouldn't be distracted by thoughts of her.

And maybe after Christmas, his life would make sense again.

Chapter Four

"No barking," Leah instructed the leashed schnauzer trotting alongside her up the circular drive to Hughes House on the Saturday morning after Thanksgiving. "Don't rip up any plants, either. This isn't my house yet. *Our* house," she clarified as the front door opened and Benton appeared in the threshold.

He met them with a grin. "This must be Ralph."

"The groomer ran late. Rather than run him home and be late meeting you, I thought he could run around the backyard while we work, since it's fenced."

"Great idea. Hey, Ralph." As she mounted the steps to the porch, Benton dropped to his haunches to introduce himself to the dog. Ralph sniffed Benton's fingers and clearly found his new friend to be okay because he nudged Benton's arm for a pat. Benton obliged, rubbing Ralph's sleek gray coat with both hands. "You just had a bath, eh, boy?"

"He's pretty proud of himself on bath day, too. Like he feels spiffy. I normally groom him myself, but I've been so behind lately."

"You've worked all week, haven't you?" He glanced up at her.

"Yes." But it had been Grandma who'd kept her up last night—not that Benton needed to be troubled with that. "Why don't I take Ralph around to the back, and then we can get to work inside the house."

"Sounds good." He went back inside the house.

Her dog eagerly pawed the path as she unlatched the gate to the backyard. "All right, just a second." Once inside the gate, she unclipped Ralph's leash and set him loose. Instead of bolting over the lush winter rye grass as she expected, however, he trotted straight to the back porch, where Benton was setting down a silver mixing bowl.

"This is the best I could find for a water dish."

He'd thought to provide Ralph with a drink? "It's perfect. And so considerate. Thanks." Her gaze took in the expansive yard. Back in the day, there must have been quite a garden here, but now it was entirely ornamental, with grass, trees and benches. Someone still took care of mowing and weeding, but the shrubs and flowers bordering the lawn all shared an overgrown look. Mature trees and the tall redwood fence blocked a view of the yard from the street.

Oddly, though, the farthest reaches of the yard, still within the boundary of the redwood fence, had been enclosed by a waist-high picket fence. Part of the enclosed area was hidden from view by cypress trees and tangled-looking bare rosebushes, but white siding was visible. A garden shed? Leah strode over the damp grass and then gasped. The fenced-off area was a backyard, and behind the cypress and roses? "There's a little house hidden back here."

"*Little* is in the eye of the beholder." Benton caught up to her, his dark eyes round with amazement. "It's a good-sized house. Larger than the one I rent."

"It makes my place look like a postage stamp." She followed Benton through the gate, walking up to the back porch of the one-story Craftsman. The house was a hundred years old, maybe, not as old as Hughes House. "I never noticed it from the street."

They walked around the house, under an old carport to the lawn in front of the house. From the street, red-wood fencing blocked the house from view, but clearly it hadn't always been that way. A driveway led straight into the fence. Weird. "Staff residence or guesthouse?"

"We'll have to ask Rowena." Benton toed the rotting porch step with his boot. "Not in the best of shape, I'm afraid."

"It's got good bones, though. And what a view, from that back porch at least. These roses must be gorgeous in summer."

Returning to the back of the house, Leah breathed heavily of the grass-scented air. What would it be like to live in this house? To take time every evening to sit on this porch in a rocking chair and bask in the sight and scent of the dewy blooms while Ralph investigated beneath every bush, as he did now?

Someday she'd have a place like this, a charming spot surrounded by trees and roses to call her own. After Grandma—well, this wasn't the time to think about that. She squared her shoulders. "Shall we get to work?"

"I'm ready." He rubbed his hands together. "Before we go too far, though, I've got something to show you."

She stopped dead on the grass. "Please don't tell me you found a rat's nest or a zillion spider babies."

Laughing, he jogged up the porch steps and opened the kitchen door for her. "No, it's a good thing. Rowena mentioned she had a scrapbook of photos from all her old Gingerbread Galas. Looking at the pictures will help a lot."

"That is a good surprise." She entered the kitchen and dropped Ralph's leash on the chipped Formica counter. "It'll be easier to plan this party if we can copy what Rowena used to do. Where is it?"

"I left it in the room with the *maroon* couch."

Cheeky man. She grinned back at him as she led the way to the front parlor. "These things are important, Benton," she teased.

Ah, there on the coffee table lay a thick, black leather-bound book from an earlier age. Leah moved the scrapbook to the center of the table, so they could sit side by side on the couch and look through it together. It felt filmy as she opened it. In daylight, it was easier to see a layer of dust on the furniture and the grimy cast to the windows. "It is pretty dirty in here."

"And cold. Nothing happened when I tried the thermostat. I'll look into it later, but if you're freezing, I can hunt for a space heater."

It was almost as cold in the house as it was outside, but she wore a quilted black jacket and thick acrylic socks beneath her boots. Besides, they wouldn't be here long. "I'm okay, but we'd better add the HVAC to our to-do list. We need heat before the party."

She turned her attention to the scrapbook. The first pages of colored photos had faded to orange-brown tones in the five plus decades since they were taken.

Benton made a wowed noise. "I don't know what's more impressive, the size of that Christmas tree or the volume of Rowena's hair."

"The beehive, definitely. Ooh, this must be her husband."

"Hyland." Benton tapped the image of the mustachioed gentleman in a ruffled tuxedo. "He passed on about fifteen years ago. Wow, high fashion in these photos."

"I'll say." The beehive hair gave way to a Farrah Fawcett style as Rowena's clothes shifted from sleek dresses to wide-legged jumpsuits. They'd reached photos of the thin necktie and shoulder pad era of the eighties when Leah sighed. "Lots of photos of guests, but I'm not seeing much detail of the party itself, other than the Christmas tree." Placed in the foyer, it was always an intimidating ten-footer, at least. She jotted it on the list.

"Yeah, the photographers were more interested in the people than the mechanics." Benton shifted against her on the couch, a completely innocent move, but one that made her aware of his closeness. "I confess I'm rudderless here. I can cook a pot of spaghetti or let someone sleep in my guest room, easy, but when it comes to something like this, I need all the concrete clues I can get to pull it off."

"There's a big difference between hospitality and gala throwing."

"I guess the most important things are blessing Rowena and the town museum fund, and offering a pleasant evening for the guests."

"You remind me of my dad." Leah didn't mean to speak it aloud, but it blurted out as a memory flooded her. "He was always reminding us to be grateful for every opportunity we had to serve, because ultimately, it's for the Lord."

"I like that perspective."

So did Leah, and she was grateful for her father's example. A wave of longing rushed over her, but this was not the time to let it sweep her away.

She tapped a photo of the dining room. "Looks like a beverage station. Looks like something lumpy in that bowl? Marshmallows?"

Benton leaned down for a closer look. The rosemary-mint smell of his shampoo swirled around her, causing her heart to ka-thump like a car stuck between first and second gear.

Shocked by her response, Leah turned her head. It wasn't like she was unaccustomed to being close enough to people that she could smell their shampoo. She was in her patients' personal spaces all the time.

But Benton was not a patient. He was single, handsome and kind to her dog.

He was also a pastor. She shifted half an inch away from him.

Benton, thankfully, seemed oblivious to her internal battle, because he grinned as he leaned back. "I think it's a hot chocolate station. Marshmallows, whipped cream, peppermint sticks, and I think that's a jar of something to sprinkle on top, like cinnamon or chocolate jimmies. I'm down for that in a big way."

He looked like a little boy at the prospect, and she couldn't blame him. "Me, too."

"Did you see this picture yet? Everyone is holding a to-go box."

Leah searched her memories. "Rowena said something about sending gingerbread people home with guests—"

A resounding trio of thumps hit the front door, sending Leah to her feet.

"Maybe it's the mayor again." Benton's neutral tone was a stark contrast to the sinking in Leah's stomach. She envied his compassion and confidence at the prospect of facing the accusatory Judy Hughes once more.

The woman at the front door wasn't the mayor, though. It was the same peach-haired woman they'd encountered when they visited Rowena's lawyer. Leah wouldn't soon forget the look of keen interest and suspicion in the older woman's eyes. What was her name again?

"Maude, what a surprise." Benton smiled.

Maude. That was it.

"I saw your car out front and I thought, how odd, surely Pastor Benton wouldn't be lollygagging around in this empty house, so I went on my way around the corner but then I saw a vicious dog in the backyard." Clutching a purple scarf around her neck, Maude pushed past him into the foyer. Her steps faltered when she caught sight of Leah. "You again."

"Hello." Leah wanted to smile but was still processing the idea that Ralph behaved viciously. He was so sweet with everyone, she often worried he'd follow someone else home. "Ralph is my dog. I'm so sorry he frightened you. What did he do, so I can correct it?"

"He sniffed at my scarf." Maude's chin jutted in the air.

How could Ralph have snuffled the woman's scarf when it was tightly wrapped around her neck, a few feet higher than the dog was tall, and when they were separated by a tall wood fence? Unless Maude bent down to peer through a gap in the fence.

"Oh, dear." Leah could only shake her head. "Again, my apologies."

"No harm done, I suppose, but mark my words, everyone in town will be talking about the strange dog and woman parading around Hughes House."

"And me, for that matter?" Benton grinned.

"Hello?" The friendly greeting drew their attention back to the open door. A slight woman dressed in athletic clothes stood in the threshold, her expression hesitant as she brushed her light brown bob behind her ear. "I'm sorry to intrude, Benton, but the door's open and I saw your car."

"No intrusion at all. Come in, Faith. Do you know Leah Dean?"

"Of course. We attend church together." Leah answered for Faith Latham, reaching for a hug. She had no idea why Benton invited Faith here, but Leah appreciated the friendly face.

"That's right." Benton gestured toward Maude. "Faith, this is a member of Good Shepherd, Maude Donalson."

Faith offered a friendly wave. "We've met at my store." Faith's Finds sold antiques on Main Street, and Faith oversaw the newly formed town museum council. Ah, was that why she was here? The Gingerbread Gala proceeds were all going to the museum fund.

"You seem to have a few lady friends at Creekside Community, don't you, Pastor Benton?" Maude's lips tightened like the mouth of a drawstring purse.

Faith shook her head. "My fiancé, Tom, attends Benton's Bible study breakfasts at Del's each Wednesday, and Benton is officiating my wedding in two months while our pastor recuperates from surgery. At premarital counseling, he mentioned helping Rowena throw one last Gingerbread Gala, and I couldn't help but stop by. These historic properties are gems."

"The Gingerbread Gala?" Maude's lips popped apart.

"Leah and I were asked to coordinate it, yes." Benton's answer was truthful, but he didn't elaborate any more than necessary. Leah appreciated his discretion. Rowena might not yet want everyone to know about her will.

"I think it's splendid." Faith's wide-eyed gaze took in the foyer and the grand staircase. "These sconces are original, I'm sure of it. And would you look at this woodwork. The newel posts are exquisite. I'm so glad no one in the Hughes family ever replaced these treasures. I wonder if the decor was vintage Victorian for the parties."

"Not unless foil icicles and bubble lights are Victorian," Maude said.

If Leah's ears were capable of perking like a dog's, they surely would have. "You attended, Maude?"

"A few times. They were always far too crowded for my tastes." Maude sniffed again. "Once there were so many people packed like sardines in the foyer, I could hardly see the gingerbread house set up here." She gestured at the marble table in the center of the room.

"Gingerbread house?" Leah and Benton spoke at the same time.

"It's called the Gingerbread Gala, isn't it?" Maude's skinny eyebrows rose.

Leah met Benton's gaze. "We thought it was called the Gingerbread Gala because Rowena sent the guests home with gingerbread cookies."

"Cookies? More like rocks, hard enough to break a tooth on. Good gingerbread is soft. Like mine. I won the blue ribbon at the county fair four times for my gingerbread." Maude held up four fingers. "But the party was named for the house, right in the center of that table so it was the first thing people saw when they came in. It's not like they were ever as fancy as the ones at the White House."

One more thing for the to-do list. A fancy gingerbread house to serve as a focal point for the whole party. Leah shrugged at Benton. "I'll call Angel Food Bakery."

"Oh, they don't do those," Maude said with another sniff. "Too time-consuming."

While Maude regaled Faith with the secret to her blue-ribbon gingerbread, Leah resolved to double-check with the bakery just in case Maude was mistaken. If they couldn't craft one, surely they could direct her to a professional… Who wouldn't mind taking on a project with only three and a half weeks to get the job done.

Panic clawed up Leah's throat. Three and a half weeks in the busiest season of the year for parties, when musicians and caterers might already be booked. She and Benton still had to handle all of that, plus clean, decorate, sell tickets and advertise. Her heart skittered in her chest, hard and fast like a rabbit's. She and Benton had full-time jobs. On top of that, he had a church to fix up and she had Grandma Clare.

She looked at Benton, hardly able to breathe. "How are we ever going to pull off this party?"

The moment the whispered words left Leah's mouth, Benton could tell she regretted them. Her hand covered her lips, but neither Maude nor Faith appeared to have overheard. When she turned and stepped into the parlor, he followed her. She was clearly in distress. The gingerbread house must have been one item too many for the long checklist.

He touched her elbow. "We can't, I don't think. But with God all things are possible. Even gingerbread houses."

Her shoulders relaxed. "I definitely need to pray."

Much as he was accustomed to doing things himself, he might have to ask for help. "Maybe we can ask friends if they'd mind helping us decorate." Of course, there was a lot to do before that, like clean the place up and fix the heater. "But right now, I think we should go talk to Rowena."

"Now, as in *now*?"

He nodded. They couldn't speak freely, what with Maude and Faith in the foyer, and a change of scenery would clear both of their minds.

"I'll meet you there. I have to drop off Ralph. I'll lock the kitchen door behind me." She picked up her purse and the scrapbook. After a quick word of farewell to Maude and Faith, she disappeared to the back of the house.

"I'm afraid I need to leave now, as well." Benton got out his key. "Thanks so much for stopping by."

As Benton, Maude and Faith stepped onto the front porch, Leah and Ralph, stubby tail wagging, rounded the side of the house. Leah waved again but didn't stop, hurrying toward her red SUV. Benton hadn't realized he'd been watching them go until Maude gripped his elbow. "I'll be sure to tell Clementine about the Gingerbread Gala."

Here we go again. "I hope she enjoys it. Tell her to

bring Wynn and Annie." Her niece and nephew. Benton twisted the key in the lock.

"Let me know how I can help," Faith said, as they headed down to the sidewalk. "This is an overwhelming job."

Overwhelming. That about sums it up, doesn't it, Lord? Benton drove the familiar roads to Creekside Retirement Village practically on autopilot, praying the entire way. *Leah seems so weighed down, and it breaks my heart. The gala is a lot of work, but there's more bothering her. I can't imagine how difficult it must be to see her grandma slip the way she is.*

He wished he could do more for Leah, but he had to be careful. They'd been thrown together by Rowena for a task, but they weren't friends. And he did his best to keep a professional boundary between himself and single women.

That said, something about Leah and her burdens hit him, and he wanted to help. Wanted her to get as much joy out of this Gingerbread Gala as she could.

Once parked, he texted Rowena—he should've thought of doing that earlier—and received an immediate response.

I have sugar-free cookies. Hurry in before I eat them all.

Leah pulled into the parking lot as he got out of the car, and he met her at her driver's side door. "Rowena's expecting us. Did Ralph get squared away?"

"He is comfy on his favorite blanket with a treat." She clutched the scrapbook to her chest. "Thanks for reminding me that God's in this. Sometimes I feel like I'm in this life all by myself, but I know that's not true."

He could see how she could feel that way. Her parents had died when she was young, and the grandmother who raised her didn't know her anymore. Leah was, in many ways, on her own. But not entirely. "He gave us each other for this project, too. Don't forget that. This isn't all on you."

She glanced at him as they entered the retirement village's lobby. "Thanks. I'm glad one of us is calm about this party."

"I'm stressed, believe me." He opened the door leading to Rowena's building. "I don't know the first thing about galas or hoedowns, but I figure whatever we do, we do. Don't get me wrong, I want to do our best. I hope it blesses Rowena, and I hope it helps Faith's museum. But in four weeks, it's over."

Rowena's apartment door was ajar, and she welcomed them inside from her perch on the couch. Benton's stomach panged at the sight of the plate of beige cookies on the coffee table. Rowena chuckled. "You have questions to ask about the gala, don't you? Have a cookie first."

It tasted like orange. "Delicious, Rowena."

"You made these?" Leah took one but didn't taste it.

"Of course not. They're the diabetic-friendly option at Angel Food Bakery."

Benton was still chewing, but when Leah's eyes widened, he knew she was on top of this. "Speaking of Angel Food, we saw Maude and she said they made the gingerbread people you gave to the guests. Did they also create your gingerbread houses for the gala?"

"Mona did."

Mona was still the owner, but since she retired her daughter Claudia ran the Main Street bakery. "Even if the bakery itself is out of the gingerbread house business, maybe Mona can help, since she's not part of the day-to-day operation."

"The gingerbread house is the focal point of the entire affair," Rowena said, making what looked like jazz hands. "I can't wait to see what it looks like this year. Ah, you found the scrapbook, I see."

"It's been fun to look at. I brought it in case you wanted to reminisce." Leah set it closer to Rowena. How kind of her. Benton had assumed she'd brought it to ask Rowena questions.

"Ah yes." Rowena opened to the first page and gasped at the photo of her husband in the ruffled shirt. "I loved that suit on Hyland."

"Handsome guy." Leah bit into her cookie.

"Rowena, while we're looking, we had a few other questions." Benton reached for a second cookie. "What sort of food did you have? And is that a hot chocolate station?"

"You and that hot chocolate station." Leah chuckled. It was nice to see her smiling and more relaxed.

A persistent buzz sounded, and with an apologetic smile, Leah pulled her phone from her purse. "Sorry, I need to check this." She stood and answered the phone. "Marigold? How are you?"

Marigold was one of Benton's parishioners, a green-thumbed widow in her eighties who just so happened to be next-door neighbors with Benton's best friend, Kellan. She was usually a cheerful lady, but whatever Marigold had to say wasn't good, because Leah's jaw tightened.

"I'm sorry," she said, as she disconnected the call.

"Marigold volunteers on Grandma's ward and I need to run over there."

"Go. I've got this."

"Thank you." She brushed past him to kiss Rowena's cheek. "See you soon."

"Poor Leah." Rowena stared after her. "Her grandmother Clare isn't well, you see."

"She shared a little with me."

"I want her to use her share of the money to get Clare the care she needs. And maybe then, Leah will begin to care for herself. She's gone too long without any fun."

"You're a sweetheart, you know that, Rowena?"

"You're not so bad yourself."

"Maybe that's why I like you so much. You don't hold my past sins against me."

One silver eyebrow rose. "You're the pastor here, aren't you? Don't you know by now what happens when sins are forgiven?"

"I do." He took hold of her bony fingers. "Thanks for the reminder."

"I wondered when you'd bring this up. I know your last experience with the Gingerbread Gala was an unsavory one."

Not the gala, per se, but the night of it, nineteen years ago. "*Unsavory* is an understatement. I plowed into your parked car as a fourteen-year-old kid who had no business getting behind the wheel. I could've killed someone."

"Now, now, no one was hurt. And I understood your reason. You were trying to prevent your brother from driving under the influence. I still don't understand why you've kept that part a secret. You let everyone think the worst of you."

Like Mayor Judy Hughes, who'd run out from the gala and who believed Benton had taken his brother's car for a joyride—hence her calling him a criminal. In truth, his brother had driven to a friend's, drunk alcohol and intended to drive home. The friend's sibling called Benton, who'd jogged over and taken the keys. Dad was no help that night. He'd already passed out from drinking, himself. Benton did the only thing he could think of at the time—drove his brother home so no one was the wiser.

Instead, he'd hydroplaned into Rowena's parked car.

When Jarod ran away from the scene, Benton held his tongue. His family might be a mess, but it was the only one he had. He'd feared what might happen if he'd exposed his brother's and dad's drinking.

"This Gingerbread Gala will be different, God willing." God could redeem all sorts of things. "But it won't be fun if the heater's broken. Do you have a contract with any services?"

He and Rowena discussed details, but he struggled to put his family out of his mind. On Thanksgiving, he'd reached out to them, but Dad was more interested in the football game and Jarod was with friends.

It was close to dinner when they finished up, but Leah hadn't returned. Benton stood to leave. "I'll let Leah know we accomplished a lot this afternoon."

"Give her my love."

"I will." But as Benton left Rowena's complex, he decided to visit the Alzheimer's ward rather than text Leah. Maybe she'd like to grab dinner. Another potpie at Del's? It sounded good on such a chilly evening.

The memory care unit was small, just a handful of rooms. The strong smell of disinfectant and the sound of someone crying met him as he greeted the nurse on staff. She directed him down the hallway to the source of the tears. Inside the room, Leah stood over the bed, comforting a rail-thin, weeping woman.

"Oh, Grandma, it's all right. I don't know what the matter is, but I'm here. It's all right."

Clare's wails hushed. "I'm so tired."

"I know. Let's get you to sleep now, shall we?" Leah assisted her grandmother back against the pillows.

Benton stepped back, hot with shame, like he was an interloper. Leah might not appreciate him barging in on such a private moment. But worse was the strange feeling churning in his gut. Envy. Not of the circumstances, but the familial love evident in Leah's tender touch and kind words. In her grandma's subsiding sobs as she let Leah tuck her into the blankets.

He wanted that sort of love. The love of a family.

First, he needed to help the family he already had. He had to get things right with them before he could have a family of his own.

Chapter Five

It might still officially be November, but now that Thanksgiving was over, it was starting to look like Christmas in Widow's Peak Creek. Leah, Irene, and other staff had switched out the decor in the skilled nursing unit, replacing the leaf garland with faux pine hung with stockings. As Leah parked her car on Main Street during her lunch break on Monday, she smiled at the jaunty red and gold bows tied around the light posts and the red tinsel snowflakes hung on garland above the road.

Walking to Angel Food Bakery, Leah peeked in all the shop windows she passed. Red bows and holly sprigs accented the snow gear in the display window of The World Outside outdoor goods. Old-fashioned electric bulbs illuminated a vintage-themed Christmas tree at Faith's antiques store, and at the crafts store, In Stitches, dolls resembling Santa's elves had been posed to look as if they were knitting scarves.

The scene was cheery and festive, but also a reminder that December was nigh, and the Gingerbread Gala would be here soon.

Leah stepped inside Angel Food Bakery, met at once by jazz-style Christmas music and the delectable coffee-and-bread aroma of the place. A few customers sat at café-style tables, and Claudia, the proprietor, was busy at the espresso machine beneath the chalkboard menu hanging on the wall. Benton had beat Leah here, and he peered into the display case at trays of fresh-baked goodies.

Her stomach did a funny flip. Surely, it wasn't because of him. More that Irene had teased her all morning about her "lunch date" with the cute pastor.

It's not much of a lunch date when you decide to eat first. In my case, scarfing a sandwich in the car.

Benton turned. "Hey. I'm getting a box of scones for the church office. Want anything?"

"I can't leave here without a chocolate-dipped macaroon."

He grinned. "You can't? Or won't?"

"Can't. Won't. It's a fact, that's all." She sidled alongside him, catching a faint whiff of his aftershave, musky and oh-so nice. Her stomach flipped again, and her hand pressed it as if she could press it into submission.

His gaze caught the movement of her hand. "You didn't get a chance to grab lunch yet? This will wait if you want to run out for a bite first."

"It was busy at work, but I managed to wolf down a peanut butter sandwich." For lack of something better to do with her hands, she shoved them into the pockets of her gray sweater. "You?"

His smile widened. "That's exactly what I ate, too. Jelly or honey on yours?"

"Raspberry jelly."

"Honey." He laughed. "But I left a lot of room for dessert."

Claudia's lips twitched at their exchange. "Hello, folks. Ready to order, Benton?"

"A dozen assorted scones, please, but make sure one is raspberry almond or Jan will give me the look of death. She's the church office manager," he explained to Leah before returning his attention to Claudia. "And two chocolate-dipped macaroons, separately packaged. Was there anything else you wanted, Leah?"

One of those macaroons was for her? She'd expected to buy her own. "No, thanks. But that's twice you've paid now. Next time is on me."

Behind the waterfall of Claudia's gray-tinged black hair, Leah glimpsed a hint of a smile. Hopefully Claudia hadn't gotten the wrong impression about Leah and Benton's relationship. They were partners planning the gala, nothing more.

But Leah well knew pastors' lives were up for public consumption, especially in a town the size of Widow's Peak Creek. Benton drew interest wherever he went, at least when she'd been with him. First his friends Kellan and Paige, then Maude and now Claudia.

"Did you want anything else?" Using plastic tongs, Claudia packaged the scones in a white cardboard box.

"Information." Benton hitched his thumb at a blackboard sign propped on the counter by the register. "I see you're not taking any special orders before Christmas."

Claudia shook her head. "I'm booked solid."

Leah wasn't ready to give up yet. "We're bringing back the Gingerbread Gala this year and we've found ourselves in desperate need of gingerbread cookies and a house. We heard your mom used to make them. If you're booked up, do you think she might be interested in helping us for the event?"

"The Gingerbread Gala's coming back? Wow, for something like that, yeah, I think so." Claudia handed Benton two white paper sleeves containing the macaroons. "If she hadn't fallen off a ladder this weekend and broken her arm."

Leah winced. "Ouch. Sorry to hear about that. Does she need anything?"

"Patience," Claudia said with a smile.

"Do you know anyone who makes gingerbread houses?" Benton handed over a bill.

"I couldn't have helped you there anyway. They're too time-consuming for me." Claudia shrugged. "Try the internet. Or make one yourselves. There's a class at the rec center on Thursday night. I posted a flyer about it on the bulletin board."

Make one themselves? Ha. Once she and Benton were seated on the park-style bench in front of Angel Food, she rolled her eyes. "Surely someone around here sells gingerbread houses."

"I'm already on it." Benton scrolled through his cell phone, looking up nearby bakeries. "Minor setback, Leah. Oof."

"Oof what?" That didn't sound encouraging. She leaned in to look at his phone.

"The bakery in Pinehurst." He tipped the phone so she could see a picture of a gingerbread house trimmed in candy and icing. "They only took preorders until Thanksgiving. We missed that boat with them, but there have to be others we can try." Benton slipped his phone into the pocket of his black jacket. "Let's take a break and enjoy our macaroons."

Leah could use the chocolate, after such downer news. "Thanks."

Benton bit into his. His eyes widened. "Mmm."

"So good, right?" Determined to savor hers, Leah nibbled it.

"I've never tried these before." He brushed crumbs from his hands. "I can see why you refuse to leave Angel Food without one."

A figure in a periwinkle blue coat halted in front of their bench. "If it isn't the con artists. I don't know how you two crooks weaseled the house out of poor aunt Rowena."

Not again. Judy Hughes, Rowena's niece by marriage, sneered down at them like they were litter left on the sidewalk. All the joy Leah felt from partaking of the most delicious cookie on earth evaporated.

"Mayor Hughes." Benton smiled. How could he do that? How could he be so nice to that woman when she continued to insult them?

Hands fisting, Leah hopped to her feet. "If you have any concerns, I suggest you speak to Rowena or her lawyer, but please don't call us derogatory names again."

"We're throwing a Gingerbread Gala this year, at Rowena's request." Benton spoke before the mayor could respond, standing as he did so. "We were just talking about the gingerbread house for the foyer. Our hope is to make the evening special for Rowena."

"It'll be an unforgettable evening, that's for sure. So many momentous things happen on the night of the Gingerbread Gala." The mayor's eyes narrowed to snake-like slits.

"Rowena will have fun, and that's all we care about." Leah folded her arms. "And since the proceeds will benefit the town museum, I'm sure you, as mayor, will be sure to show support."

"I'll want to see paperwork. Ensure the funds go to the right place."

As if they'd steal the gala proceeds. Leah's vision darkened, but Benton's hand on her arm kept her from losing her cool.

"We're working directly with Faith and the museum council." His voice was smooth as velvet. "Every dime will go right where Rowena wants it to."

With a harrumph, the mayor shoved past them into the bakery.

Leah shook her head. "You are truly a man of peace, Benton. I don't know how you keep your cool."

"Practice, I guess." His tone was light, but at once she remembered that his father and brother had problems with alcohol. It was entirely possible Benton had to play peacemaker in his family when he was growing up.

Heart aching, she reached for his arm. Then pulled it back before she made contact. "She shouldn't call us those names, though. Criminal? Anyway, how should we handle looking for a gingerbread house? I can get online tonight." She had nothing to do besides hang out with Ralph and watch TV, anyway.

"Why don't we take that class at the rec center? It's only two days away, and if it's helpful, we can make the house ourselves. If not, we'll still have time to call every bakery from Tahoe to San Francisco. Making a house ourselves takes time, sure, but so does traveling out of town to get one and transport it back."

Sounded fair. "All right. In the meantime, we should figure out how to sell tickets and make flyers."

"Show me the to-do list."

It only took a few seconds for them to divide a few tasks between them.

Benton glanced at his watch. "Time to go back to work, so I'll see you Thursday at the rec center. In the meantime, don't let the mayor get you down, okay?"

"Okay."

"Or anything else."

Like Grandma? She hadn't told Benton how agitated Grandma had been on Saturday, but she couldn't help feeling like he knew somehow. "I'll try."

"I'm praying. For you, the gala, all of it." He scooped his box of scones off the bench. "See you Thursday."

"Looking forward to it."

It was a turn of phrase, a polite thing to say. But the truth was, she was looking forward to more time with Benton. As friends, of course. Nothing more.

But the tiny flip in her stomach had nothing to do with him being her friend.

Thursday night, Benton rushed into the concrete block recreation center and followed the sounds of conversation and holiday music to the large room at the end of the hall. It reminded him of a school lunchroom with its large windows, fluorescent lighting, linoleum floor and the faintest whiff of bleach permeating the air. And like a school lunchroom, it was full of chatting people.

They gathered around rectangular tables in groups, except for Leah, the only individual alone in the room. Alone at one end of a table, she wore a gray turtleneck sweater, and her dark hair was pulled into a messy bun. She didn't notice his arrival, with her gaze fiercely fixed on a tube of something like toothpaste.

"Sorry I'm late." Benton dropped into the cold metal

folding chair across from her. "Pageant rehearsal ended on schedule, but then someone dropped in."

Her brows met in concern. "If you need to be with a parishioner, it's okay. I've got this."

"Nothing like that." He shrugged out of his black wool peacoat. "It was Odell. Maude's son. He wanted to check on my progress with the parish hall." Benton was almost finished with the stage steps and had purchased the necessary tools to patch up the damaged linoleum, but Odell insisted Benton had promised to paint the place, too. Benton hadn't recalled that being part of the initial agreement, but he'd deal with it later. Right now, he had something else on his plate.

"Are you sure? Do you need to go back?" Leah looked up. "My dad was a pastor, remember? There was always something coming up at the last minute."

"Nope, it's all good." Or it would be. "Looks like we have all we need." He gestured at foot-by-foot panels of gingerbread on the table, stamped with lines marking the door and windows. Benton picked up one of the smaller pieces, a side wall, by the look of it. The gingerbread looked more like cardboard than a bakery item. It probably tasted like wood pulp, too. Good thing there were paper bowls of candy and cereal decorations he could nibble.

"All the materials, yes, but the instructions? Not so much. The instructor gave us a quick rundown and then put the Nat King Cole Christmas album on over the loudspeakers. This is all on us."

"Doesn't look too hard." At least, everyone else seemed to be managing fine.

"I'm starting to glue the walls together with this squeeze frosting. I don't know if I'm using the right amount. We need enough to make the pieces stick, but not so much that it oozes everywhere."

"I have no clue what amount is right, but that looks good." Not too much icing, not too little. "Want me to hold it in place while the icing hardens up?"

"Sure."

Their fingers brushed during the handoff and Benton's neck got hot. He concentrated on the gingerbread while she hurriedly iced the roof.

"There." She lowered it into place, and they held the panels in position, waiting for the icing to dry. "I've never done this part of a gingerbread house. Just the fun part."

"Decorating? Or eating?" With one hand holding the panels in place, he snatched a black gumdrop from one of the paper bowls.

"Ew, you like the black ones?"

"Licorice? It's awesome."

"Red licorice, yes." She took a length of Red Vines and waved it at him. "But when it comes to gumdrops, it's got to be cherry."

"Is that what the red ones are? It's always hard to tell what sort of fruit they are. Cherry, strawberry, generic berry."

"Delicious, is what they are."

"So, we agree on potpie and macaroons but not on gumdrops."

"More generic berry-red ones for me, then."

"Speaking of candy." Using a Red Vine as a pointer, he gestured at the gingerbread house. "Where should we put them?"

She craned her neck and looked around. "Those people have Red Vines on the roof of their house. It looks cute, like a cheery little rain gutter. Want to do that?"

He'd never think of red licorice the same way again. "Sure. What about the Froot Loops?"

She held a green one up to the stamped door. "Too small for a wreath. How about we put them together to form a path to the door?"

"Blue ones for windows?" Even though they were circular, he could clump a group together.

"Why not. Too bad we don't have any wafer cookies for shutters. I think the house is ready to decorate, if we don't push too hard and knock it down." She let go of the panels she'd been holding together. "Hey, it didn't fall over."

"See? We've got this."

They took turns dabbing candy and cereal into the icing and gluing it on the gingerbread walls, chatting as they worked. Leah was crafting a green gumdrop bush when she looked up. "Did you get a chance to set up the website for the gala tickets?"

"Took less than ten minutes." He had some experience with ticketing apps due to church activities. "The site is ready to go live but I wanted to make sure I checked with you first. I took a picture on my phone if you want to see it." He pulled it up and showed her.

"Date, time and price all look right. There's the mention of the town museum fund. Nice job. It can go live tonight, or whenever it's convenient for you. The flyers are printed and ready to distribute. Tomorrow I'll drop by Angel Food and hang one on the community board. Maybe you could take some to spread the news?" She pulled a paper bag from her purse and withdrew a short stack.

"Absolutely." The flyers had a festive look, with full-color graphics of holly and a gingerbread house. "These are fabulous, Leah."

She brushed off the praise with a wave of Red Vine. "I put a notice in the county newspaper, too. It should run in the Upcoming Events section on weekends and every day online."

"Great idea. Thanks."

"Hopefully, word of mouth will help, too."

Maude had done her part sharing the news. It seemed like half the congregation knew already. "I mentioned a decorating party next Saturday, and Kellan and Paige offered to help."

"Irene did, too, with her boyfriend, Phil. We have some good friends, don't we? Too bad none of them know how to make a professional gingerbread house." Leah sighed at their gingerbread house. "No offense."

He thought about pretending to be insulted for about half a second, but he couldn't stop himself from laughing. "Nope. This is cute, but we can't use a house like this as a centerpiece for the gala. It's too small."

"And, how to say this?" She gestured at the clumps of neon-bright cereal rings plastered to the walls. "Like a Candyland game exploded."

They both laughed hard enough that the people at the other end of the table looked at them. They were smiling, though. Everyone was smiling. How could they not be happy, surrounded by candy and classic Christmas tunes? "I haven't thought of that game in a million years."

"Surely you're not that old." A red gumdrop slowly slid off the roof. She popped it into her mouth.

"Not quite." Felt like it sometimes. Not tonight,

though. He followed her lead and swiped a drip of icing with his thumb, which he promptly licked off. "Mmm, that's good stuff."

"The good news about our pathetic house here is now we're cleared to look elsewhere for the gala's gingerbread house." Laughing, she reached for another Red Vine and bit off the end.

"About that."

The vertical crease between her eyes appeared, a sign she was concerned. "Why do I feel like you're about to say we're not going with a professionally made house now?"

"Hear me out. I know we agreed to wait and see how this went, but I admit it, I looked online. The only bakery within a two hours' drive that makes gingerbread houses only does ones around this size. The big fancy types are special order, and we're too late. I think we're stuck making one."

"Benton." She waved her Red Vine like a floppy pointer. "Look at this."

"It's cute."

"It's not gala material."

"This is not the best we can do, though. This was our first try. I think we can pull something off."

"I guess if we can't find one to buy, that's that." She sat back, folding her arms. "We're going to have to do research. And look at pictures for inspiration because free-form isn't going to cut it. It's also going to have to be bigger, if it's going to stand out on that marble table. Like a two- or three-story gingerbread house."

"Like Hughes House."

Her eyes widened. "A miniature Hughes House?"

Honestly, he hadn't mentioned Hughes House because he thought it would be a fun idea for a model. He was thinking in terms of its size and structure. But now that she'd said it, it wasn't just a fun idea. It was the *only* idea. "Rowena would love it. Can we try?"

"She would like it, wouldn't she?"

"Let's go for it. Tell me how big it should be, and I'll make up a pattern for the gingerbread pieces. I'll even make the gingerbread. I might need to borrow a mixer or something."

"I have a stand mixer. And my oven's big. I'll bake it."

"Then I'll buy the candies and stuff to decorate it."

"How will we make it look like Hughes House, though? I mean, rather than a three-story Greek Revival house? It's got to be Hughes House."

Benton dug through the gumdrop bowl for another black one. "Leave that to me."

"Are you sure about this?" She fiddled with her necklace. "Not the part about you buying candies. I mean the whole thing."

"Not just the house, but the gala?" At her nod, he understood. "It's a lot. You know, tomorrow I'll look at more options for the house. I'm sure I missed a bakery out there."

"No, I think we should make it. It'll be fun, and I want to surprise Rowena. It's just…life can get overwhelming sometimes."

"How's your grandma?"

"She's—the same. Thanks for asking. Saturday evening wasn't so great for her. She wanted to walk outside, but it was getting dark already, even if there was enough staff for someone to go accompany her. She needs to be somewhere that's better equipped to handle her need to wander."

"As soon as Hughes House sells, you'll get her there. But until then, I'll be praying for her."

"I appreciate that." Her eyes looked watery, but she blinked back any tears that might have fallen. "All right, enough serious stuff. Want to take home our ginger-bread wreck?"

"No, you take it."

"Ralph might eat it. Then again, maybe not even he would want this." She laughed as another gumdrop slid off the roof.

They spent a few minutes coordinating their sched-ules, nibbling on the gingerbread house until the rec center was all but empty. Benton hadn't noticed other people leaving. "I'll walk you to your car."

He ended up with the nibbled-on gingerbread house, and once he returned to his place around the corner from the church, he plopped it on the kitchen bar where he normally ate his breakfast. His first piece of Christ-mas decor, and looking at it made him smile.

Was this what life could be like if he were open to a relationship? Laughing with someone over silly things like which flavor of gumdrops was better? Working as a team?

Maybe. But he wasn't open to it. Couldn't be.

Nevertheless, he whistled a Christmas carol as he went about his evening chores.

Chapter Six

"This is for you." Leah held out a paper cup of hot chocolate to Benton as he walked up the sidewalk toward her after work the following Friday.

"For me? Thanks. What prompted this?"

She led the way into the fenced-off parking lot at the north end of town that Taylor Tree Farms used to sell their trees. "You paid last time, and it's a well-known fact you can't shop for a Christmas tree without hot chocolate."

"Actually, you can."

"But why would you want to?" Shifting her gaze away from Benton's handsome grin, she took in the assortment of firs, spruces and pines. "It's a good thing we got here when we did. People buy trees right after Thanksgiving, and already the selection's not as good as I hoped."

Benton half choked on his hot chocolate. "You're joking, right? We're surrounded by a hundred trees, at least."

"Not in the size we need. Rowena's foyer needs a ten-to-twelve-footer. Not just to fill the space, either.

We need a big, pretty tree to distract people from our homemade gingerbread house," she teased.

"The bigger the better, then," Benton teased back. A gust of wind hit, ruffling his hair into charming disarray. Unbothered, he drank his hot chocolate, then pointed with his cup. "Those back there look like they have potential."

Sure enough, there looked to be a few at the back of the lot that might fit the bill. Weaving her way through the fresh-smelling trees, Leah pulled her coat lapels tighter around her. The chill wind felt as if it blew right off the snow capping the Sierra Nevada Mountains, penetrating to her bones. Her skinny jeans tucked into black boots might look cute, but they weren't her warmest fashion choices.

Benton caught her shiver and tugged his plaid scarf from around his neck. "Here."

It took two seconds to find her tongue. "Don't you need it?"

"Nah, I'm hot-blooded." He looped it loosely around her shoulders.

"Thank you." She adjusted the warm wool tighter about her throat. It smelled like aftershave, citrusy and beguiling, and—oh, she needed to stop it. Benton's kind gesture was intended to keep her warm, not send her into a swoon.

Clearing her throat, she pointed at the closest giant-sized tree. "How's that one right there?"

It had been eight days since they made a gingerbread house at the class. Since then, they'd continued gala preparations, but separately. Between his evening meetings, the food drive and buying paint for the parish hall, Benton measured Hughes House and bought lights to go outside, as well as a few outdoor light displays that he could stick in his front yard later. He'd created a template for the gingerbread house Leah could use as a pattern and also handled the heater repairs, so Hughes House was cozy and warm when she met with a team of house cleaners on Saturday while he officiated a wedding. While the house was deep cleaned down to the drapes, Leah shopped for decorations with Irene, and she enlisted Irene's boyfriend, Phil, a middle school music teacher, to play piano for the party. He did such a great job playing for the seniors on his monthly visits to the retirement village, so he was the perfect choice. Leah rented chairs for the music room, flutes for sparkling apple cider and mugs for the hot chocolate station. Benton hired the caterer alone on a night when she was supposed to join him, but Grandma had fallen from bed and Leah couldn't bear to leave her.

Benton had promised to pray—and to ensure stuffed mushrooms were on the menu. Later that night he'd texted her a photo of the list of appetizers to be served, and he'd circled the mushrooms. Unfortunately, the caterer didn't offer gingerbread cookies, so they still had to handle that matter.

And in the meantime, people were buying tickets. Lots of tickets. The reality that dozens of townsfolk would be there made Leah's stomach pinch with nervousness. What if the guests were bored? What if Rowena was disappointed? Was there something missing from their plans?

God, help. What is it that's missing, and how can I fix it? We want this party to bless Rowena and everyone else, and I'm so afraid it won't be good enough.

Praying was all she could do besides tackling her

half of the tasks. And while God hadn't led her to any firm conclusions about what might be lacking at the gala, she and Benton had done well getting other things done on their own time.

One thing they needed to do together, though, was the Christmas tree. Leah had the better car to transport it and Benton had the biceps. Not that she'd ever tell him that.

Studying the tree she'd pointed out, Benton rubbed his chin. "I'm not sure it's tall enough. I thought we'd go bigger. What about that one?"

Leah walked around a Colorado Blue Spruce. Nice color and scent, but—nope. "It's got a hole on this side."

"We can just turn that side to the wall, can't we?"

"If someone goes up the stairs and looks down at it, it'll look funny."

"Good point. Okay, how's that one? It's nice and full." His head tipped to the side. "Too wide, maybe. It has to fit in that space by the marble table."

"Yeah, I think you're right."

A stroller curved around the wide tree, pushed by a young couple she recognized as Benton's good friends Kellan and Paige Lambert. "Oh, hello."

"Hey there." Kellan and Benton thwacked each other on the back in that way men had of greeting each other. After a quick word with Paige, Leah peered down in the stroller. A tiny baby in a fluffy pink outfit with teddy bear ears on the hood blinked up at her with wide, dark eyes.

"She's precious." Round, pink cheeks. Little hands encased in cozy mittens. A mouth like a rosebud.

"She just started smiling a few days ago. Can you smile for Leah, Poppy?" Paige bent down and stroked the baby's full cheek. The baby responded by blossoming into a toothless grin.

"Hi, pretty girl." Leah loved babies. Always had since she'd tucked in her baby dolls at night. One day maybe she'd have one of her own. If God allowed, of course. Babies and husbands weren't things she dared dream about until she got Grandma settled.

But that didn't mean she couldn't appreciate a darling infant when she saw one.

"She likes you," Kellan said.

"I'm sure she likes everyone," Leah countered with a chuckle.

"Me best, though. Right, Poppy?" Benton squatted by the stroller and played with Poppy's feet.

Gurgling, the baby grinned again. And then hiccuped, which made them all laugh.

Kellan shoved his hands in his pockets. "Looking for a tree for the gala?"

At Benton's nod, Paige clapped. "We have our tickets. Babies are welcome, right?"

"Of course." With a final pat to Poppy's feet, Benton stood back up.

"We're coming to help decorate tomorrow," Paige told Leah.

Benton had mentioned inviting them, and Leah found herself looking forward to getting to know Paige better. "Thank you. We're decorating the tree tonight, but everything else needs a lot of work."

Poppy fussed, drawing every eye. Paige pushed the stroller back and forth. "She doesn't like it when we stand still for too long. We'd better get moving, but we'll see you tomorrow."

"Bye." Leah and Benton moved off in the opposite direction. "What nice people."

He absently fingered a pine branch. "They're practically family to me."

Oh, yes—he'd spent Thanksgiving with them, rather than his dad and brother. Did he miss his family? Leah certainly missed hers, especially at Christmas. The holidays were so joyous when Mom and Dad were alive. After that, Grandma had done her best to give Leah and her brothers happy celebrations. Which reminded her, she had news for Benton.

"I spoke with Rowena, and she'd like to be at the house for part of the decorating party. Since Grandma's had a few good days in a row, we thought it might be good for Grandma to come, too. She may not know who we are or what we're doing, but I think she'll enjoy it."

Benton's smiling eyes were darker than the hot chocolate in her cup. "Then we'd better pick a tree and start decorating so she can enjoy it tomorrow."

They discussed the pros and cons of a few more trees before he found one so perfect, it was difficult to believe it was real. Nice conical shape, good height and strong branches chock-full of dark green needles.

The tag read *Fraser Fir, eleven feet*. "The price isn't bad for such a pretty tree." Leah brushed the needles, releasing its rich, pine scent. "It's so fresh."

"No holes around the back, either." Benton met her gaze. "Is this the one, then?"

The one. Even though they were talking trees, not romance, her stomach felt hot. And not from the cocoa.

He was good with babies, thoughtful of grandmas, considerate of her being cold, godly and handsome. And that twinkle in his dark eyes?

It was almost enough to make her forget her no-pastor rule.

Almost. He was not for her. But whomever he married should count herself blessed.

"Yep." Her voice sounded a little tight. "You're the one. I mean, you found the one. It. The tree."

"All right then." Benton waved down one of the tree lot employees. "Let's get it home."

Home. More than a house, a place of love and laughter. For a moment, just a moment, she allowed herself to wish she were free to build a home, a family, with someone. With *the* one. Someone who might be a little like Benton.

But right now, a home and family were nothing but sugarplum dreams.

Home. Benton wished he could bite his tongue the moment the word left his lips and a look of something akin to shock flickered across Leah's features, fleeting but unsettling, to say the least. Did she think he'd meant to imply it was their house? Together?

Even though an hour had passed, and technically the house was theirs, once the gala was over, anyway, he was still kicking himself. Figuratively, at least, since he couldn't accomplish the actual deed while lying on the cold tile floor in the Hughes House foyer, tightening screws through the tree stand into the trunk.

"It's leaning a little bit. Stop for a second while I fix it." Leah's feet shuffled a few inches and the tree wiggled above him. "Okay, go ahead."

The tree's lowest branches tickling his ears, Benton tightened until the trunk felt good and secure. "Is it good?"

"Yes." Leah sounded excited, which made Benton feel a little better. Whatever unpleasant thing Leah had thought of back at the tree lot seemed to be over with now. "I'll get some water."

Her boot steps tapped down the hall while Benton climbed out from beneath the tree. By the time Leah returned, he'd tied the strings of a white lace tree skirt around the base.

Leah knelt to pour water into the base. "You were right. This tree was the one. I just hope I bought enough lights for it."

"I thought we were using Rowena's decorations." He glanced at the boxes he'd hauled out of the attic the other day, now sitting on the foyer floor.

"We are. Tuesday evening while you had pageant rehearsal, I tested the lights. Not all the strands worked, so I ended up buying new ones. They're in the kitchen."

"Let's get them on the tree."

She fetched them while he brought in a ten-foot ladder from the garage. When he returned, she'd climbed the stairs and was leaning over the banister, wrapping lights around the top. Once he was atop the ladder, they took opposite sides of the tree, weaving strands of white, LED fairy lights deep into the branches and out to the tips. "This is how my mom used to do it," Leah said. "It uses a lot of lights, but I like it."

He liked it too, but it was taking a while. "How long does it take you to fix up your tree at home?"

"Not long because I get a short tree. I bring Grandma a miniature tree, too. I tried a fake tree for her a few years ago, thinking I could store it in the closet, but she missed the smell. How about you? Do you put a lot of lights and ornaments on your tree?"

He went down two rungs. "I don't have a tree."

She gaped at him. "That's terrible. You need one."

"It's just me at my house."

"It's just me and Ralph at mine, but we like our tree. It makes the house feel festive."

He'd never had a tree like this, at least not in his memory. "Why not? I'll get one, but I'm not going to decorate it until the gala is done."

Leah couldn't bend any farther over the banister, so she came down the stairs. "I'll help you, if you need it."

"I probably will, because my side of the tree isn't nearly as good as yours. How about the night after the gala? The twenty-second? If we're not exhausted, that is."

"I'm never too exhausted to decorate a tree." She picked up an ornament from one of the boxes. "It's a date. I mean, a decorating date—er, deal. Let's finish these lights."

Once the lights were satisfactory to her, they trimmed the tree with Rowena's ornaments, picking and choosing among the boxes. Gold globes, lace doily angels and tiny toys hanging from gold cord gave the tree a classic look. Leah was a master of crafting bows and garland from the yards of red and gold velvet ribbon they found, and Benton climbed the staircase to get the best angle to perch a gold-gowned angel atop the tree.

Leah stood back and examined their handiwork. "Looks good to me. I'm going to buy a few more strands of lights."

"For the tree?" It was bright enough, in his opinion.

"For the banister, to go with the pine garlands Irene is bringing tomorrow. Other than that, I think we're ready for our friends to help us decorate the house tomorrow. Why don't we leave out the ornament boxes in case we decide to hang a few on garlands or cluster into glass hurricanes? Do you think Rowena would like to see her ornaments displayed all over the house like that? I want her to be happy."

And that right there was yet another reason he liked Leah. This wasn't about Leah's ego or even her decorating preferences. It was about Rowena and what would please her. "I'm sure she'll like anything you do."

"She's been so excited. I have to admit, now that we've got the tree up even I am looking forward to the party now." She adjusted one of the lace angels.

"You weren't?"

"You were?" She laughed. "No, you're right. It's going to be fun, but I was focusing on the task list, not the party itself. We don't have gingerbread cookies lined up yet, but with God's help, we've accomplished a lot."

Her smile slipped then, and the vertical crease formed between her eyes. That meant trouble. "What's bothering you?"

"Nothing concrete, but I feel like something's missing."

"Did we forget to do something on the list?"

"No, more like we're forgetting something entirely. I've been praying about it but so far I'm clueless."

He was about to ask about her concerns when his cell phone buzzed. Odell Donalson.

Jan in the office tells me you haven't started painting yet. Shouldn't you start? It will not do if the hall reeks of paint fumes on Christmas Eve.

"Everything okay?" Leah glanced at his phone.

"Yep." Benton texted a reply, stating he'd taped off

the edges and would start painting Monday. It would get done. It had to. He might not have all the paint supplies ready, but he could continue to work on other matters. "I should probably head to the parish hall, if we're done here."

"I think everything is ready for tomorrow, yes." Leah gasped. "Oh! I forgot to tell you. The house at the other end of the backyard? I asked Rowena, and it was a staff house. The last occupants were a family with four kids. The youngest daughter still lives in the area and is coming to the gala."

"No way. I'm sure she'll want to see the house. The outside, at least." Benton caught his lip between his teeth. "I'll be sure to clean off the back porch tomorrow, since it's visible from the backyard. The other guests might wander over to see it, anyway."

"I hadn't thought of that, but I'd better decorate it, too." Leah shooed at him. "You go on, but I'm going to run out there before I leave. I want to see the space so I can pick up a few decorations for tomorrow."

"I'll go with you."

"I'm fine, and you have to get to church."

"Not this second, I don't."

It had grown dark and considerably cooler since they brought in the tree, and neither had thought to don their coats, or the scarf she'd returned to him once they arrived at the house. That would speed this along, then. They both utilized the flashlight apps on their phones, hurrying over the damp grass to the staff house.

There wasn't much he could do about its need for paint, but he could rid it of cobwebs and hang lights tomorrow.

"A wreath on the door, and some lanterns on the

porch. I know just the thing." Leah's face glowed, not just from the light of her phone, but with rapture. "This is the most precious house. I love it."

"It's a lot like Kellan and Paige's house. Same vintage. Lots of character."

"I hope whoever buys Hughes House takes good care of it." Leah sounded wistful.

"Me, too." They started back to the house, arms folded against the chill as they strode over the damp grass. "Maybe let a family live in it again. The fenced-off stretch of yard is huge, just begging for kids to run around in it."

"Kids." Leah stopped in her tracks. "That's it."

"What about kids?"

"We haven't thought about the kids who are coming to the gala. We're not expecting hordes, but I've heard people talk about their kids coming, like Faith and Tom."

What bothered her? "You don't want their kids here?"

"No, I'm thrilled they'll attend, but what if they're bored to tears? Singing carols is fun, hot chocolate and gingerbread cookies are definitely fun, but adult conversation and appetizers at a fundraiser for a museum? Not so much." She gestured emphatically. "Now that I know what's been bugging me, my prayer has been answered, but I don't know what to do about it."

"We do a lot of family-friendly things at church, but my usual go-tos of a bounce house, petting zoo, craft station or taco truck won't be appropriate, right?" he joked.

She laughed. "Maybe not for a fancy holiday event in a historic house. Hmm."

"What?"

"*Historic.* Maybe we can offer some sort of old-fashioned type activity for the kids. I'll ask Faith if she has ideas about vintage games. We could set it up in the music room, couldn't we? It's empty, otherwise."

"That's a great idea. Perfect for the Dickens Christmas we talked about, back on that first night."

"I'd love it if kids caught some of the wonder I feel when I'm in this house. We'll have some things I mentioned. Food. Carol singing, and now maybe vintage games. Alas, that's as Dickens-ish as we can get. No costumed carolers, no sleigh rides through the snow."

Benton snapped his fingers. "That's it. Snow."

Leah frowned. "Snow. At the gala."

His only response was to smile down at her and quirk a brow.

"It doesn't snow in Widow's Peak Creek, Benton."

"That doesn't mean it *can't.*"

Leah's eyes widened. "Are you suggesting what I think you're suggesting?"

Oh, yeah, he was. "This is going to be so much fun. Come on."

The parish hall could wait a little longer.

Chapter Seven

Snow, in Widow's Peak Creek.

Well, foam snow, blown out of a machine, but still. Leah, for one, couldn't wait. She and Benton had decided to keep their plan a secret, so Rowena and the guests would be surprised.

Saturday, she and Benton exchanged more than one secret smile over it while they decorated Hughes House, but didn't say a word around their friends who'd come to pitch in with the work.

Leah and Benton saved most of the work for themselves, though. They'd met at Hughes House early, just the two of them, to get started. They'd decorated the staff house's porch with lanterns and greenery, then tackled Hughes House's front porch, wrapping thick red ribbon around the columns so they looked like peppermint sticks.

They'd barely finished when their friends arrived to help. Irene, Paige and Faith helped inside, while Benton, Kellan, Irene's boyfriend, Phil, and Faith's fiancé, Tom, took care of the light displays and hanging lights outside. Near midday Leah started a pot of coffee and left to buy deli sandwiches, drinks and cookies for lunch, including some diabetic-friendly dessert options for Rowena. Before returning to Hughes House, though, she'd stopped by CRV to pick up Rowena and Grandma, who was thankfully having a good day. Her short hair might resemble a frizzled mop because she refused to have it combed, but she was dressed in a petal-pink sweat suit and eager for a ride in the car.

Hopefully, today would bring her a bit of holiday cheer.

After dropping off the lunch foods in the kitchen, Leah ensured Grandma was comfortable in a plush armchair in the parlor, tucking a crocheted blanket around her lap. "All right there, Grandma? Are you warm enough?" The parlor was snug and warm, now that the heater was fixed, but Grandma had become fragile over the past year, bone-thin from her lack of appetite.

"Quite cozy." Grandma absently fingered the blanket. From here, she could see the Christmas tree in the foyer, as well as watch as the parlor was decorated. "What a pretty house."

Grinning like a child, Rowena lowered herself into the adjacent armchair. "Thank you, Clare. Leah has done a wonderful job making the house ready for my big party."

"Leah?" Grandma's tone indicated she didn't know anyone by that name.

"I'm right here." Leah didn't elaborate. Grandma didn't recognize her often, and she may have already forgotten Leah's explanation for why they'd come today. It didn't matter if Grandma knew her or not, if she was content.

Grandma returned her focus on the small crowd of

people buzzing about. Faith Latham set up vintage-looking battery-powered candles in the windowsills, nested in faux pine sprigs and bows. Irene sat cross-legged on the floor, weaving red ribbon and light strands into fragrant pine garlands, and Paige Lambert chatted with them from her spot in the foyer, filling glass hurricanes with tiny glass ornaments to use as tabletop displays. It was more activity than Grandma had been around in a while, but Leah was relieved she didn't seem agitated by the noise and movement.

"I left the sandwiches in the kitchen, whenever you all want lunch." Leah plugged in her hot glue gun near the tea tray so she could affix bows onto the stack of artificial wreaths they'd hang on mirrors and the front windows. The hot metal smell mingled in the air alongside the fragrances of pine and the coffee she'd set out for the older ladies, to go with their cookies. "I know you ate already, Rowena, but if you want something, I can get it for you."

"Just the cookies." Rowena reached for the plate. "Sugar free, I take it?"

"They are indeed."

"Christmas cookies? Yes, please." Grandma eagerly grabbed two.

Irene exchanged a smile with Leah. She knew how little Grandma ate these days.

"I want to finish what I'm doing before I eat," Faith said.

"Me, too." Irene looked up. "We should have music. Too bad Phil is outside with the guys, or he could play piano for us."

Grandma loved music. Leah didn't have much in the

way of holiday tunes on her phone, though. "Does anyone have Christmas music?"

"I do." Paige strode in from the foyer, baby Poppy fast asleep in a black fabric wrap tied around her torso. "Poppy likes good old-fashioned carols when she's cranky."

"As do I." Rowena grinned.

Paige set up her phone on the coffee table, the volume exactly right to add cheer, but not so loud that they couldn't continue to talk. The parlor filled with song, and the atmosphere became even more festive. The gluing took no time at all, and as Leah unplugged the glue gun, she patted Rowena's shoulder. "If it's all right, I'm going to work on the banister now. Holler if you need anything."

"We're fine, dear."

More than fine. Grandma sang along to "Deck the Halls" without missing a single word. Funny how music could reach places in the human mind that other things—or familiar faces—couldn't, but Leah had learned musical memory isn't always affected by Alzheimer's.

Thank You, Lord, for giving Grandma this gift. She's enjoying the holiday season and she's happy.

He'd proven His love to her so many times, especially in her darkest moments. When she lost her parents, He'd provided Grandma to care for her and her brothers. He'd given Leah a good job, the best dog in the world, and soon, the proceeds from the sale of this house. Through Rowena, God was providing the means for Leah to move Grandma to the facility on the coast.

Thank You for helping us through this gala, Lord. Every step of the way, You've been there. It hasn't been easy at times, but I'm so grateful for this opportunity, because it's from You. It's Your way of helping me get Grandma more care.

Faith laughed over something Irene said, and Leah felt a pang. Faith was her friend, but Leah had purposely kept their relationship shallow. Not just with Faith, either, but other women. Acquaintances, gals to lunch with, someone to sit with in church, sure. But friends she could trust enough to be vulnerable with? Vulnerable enough that those people could turn around and hurt her? No way. She'd learned the hard way, when she was bullied as a kid by a group of girls from church that she'd thought were friends.

Since then, she'd been closed off, except to a select few like Irene. She'd thought she was protecting herself, but had she gone too far? Because these people here were kind, gracious and generous, pitching in to help her and Benton.

Was God opening her eyes to the opportunities for deeper friendships she'd missed in Widow's Peak Creek? She was going to move away soon, but in the future, she'd pray about how and when to be more vulnerable with the friends she had yet to make. She didn't want to feel this sort of regret again about not getting to know people better.

In her remaining time, she could at least show her gratitude to those who'd come to help her today. Leah joined Paige in the foyer, stopping to admire the ornament-filled glass hurricanes Paige set out over the circular marble table. "Those look great."

"That's nice of you to say, because I have no idea what I'm doing. Most of my crafts are ones I do with the preschoolers in my class." Paige, Leah had learned, taught part-time at the preschool. "Did you want a few of these to go here on this marble table?"

"That's where the gingerbread house will go. If it turns out okay, that is. Benton and I are making it, and our first attempt was terrible."

"I'm sure it wasn't."

"There was a gumdrop avalanche off the roof."

Paige laughed. "Gingerbread houses are supposed to be fun. It's going to be beautiful, I'm sure of it, but no matter what, it'll bring a smile, and that's most important."

"You're so sweet to say that." Leah mounted the staircase with a package of plastic hooks. As she placed them every few feet apart on the banister, she couldn't ignore the welling of deep gratitude in her heart. *Thank You for this good day, Lord.*

"Everything's going to be great. It'll be a memorable evening, for sure."

"That's my prayer." Not just for Rowena, but all the people who'd bought tickets and chatted to her about it at church, work and even the grocery store. Recalling their enthusiasm brought a smile to her face.

So did Benton, striding in through the front door with Kellan, Phil and Tom, their booming voices happy and their cheeks flushed from the cold.

Benton's smile widened when his gaze met hers. Dressed in jeans and a green university sweatshirt that made his eyes look even darker than usual, he bounded up the stairs toward her.

"The front yard lights are done."

"And they look awesome, if we say so ourselves." Kellan dropped a kiss on his wife's temple. "These look great, too, honey."

"Why don't we take them into the dining room? At least one of them is for the hot chocolate station." Paige scooped up one while Kellan took two.

"There are sandwiches in the kitchen, Tom," Faith called from the parlor.

"You're speaking my language." Rubbing his stomach, Tom headed in that direction as Irene strode in from the parlor, carrying the garland she'd been working on.

"Ready for a sandwich, Irene?" Phil asked, brushing his black hair from his brow.

"Go ahead. I'll be right there." Irene set down the garland at the bottom of the stairs. "Ready for this, Leah?"

"Yes, ma'am. Let's start at the bottom and work up?"

Benton went downstairs with her. "Is that your grandma I hear singing, Leah?"

"It is." Grandma's voice wasn't as strong as it once was, nor was she quite in tune or on time, but she sang every word of "Joy to the World." The third verse, even. "I don't know all those words by heart like she does."

"She's doing so well today, Leah." Irene helped Leah secure one end of the garland to a hook on the banister. "I mean, she's happy and eating. Five of those cookies so far. Maybe you don't need to move away after all."

Benton met Leah's gaze, but didn't say anything. It was almost like he could tell what she was thinking. Like he'd seen the spear of pain that pierced her at Irene's words. Irene was a nurse, too, and knew Alzheimer's patients experienced highs and lows, but her friend was also an optimist who looked for sunshine long past nightfall.

"Music definitely helps her mood." Leah ascended

a few steps with the garland. "I bought her a radio, but it can't be on all day without disrupting other patients." One of the reasons she was moving Grandma somewhere else was for the opportunity for music therapy. "I'm glad she's enjoying herself today."

"Rowena is, too." Benton allowed the garland to drape. "Is this a good length?"

"A little more," Leah answered, peering over the banister. "There. Perfect." She affixed a fluffy bow onto the banister to hide the hook.

"I think everyone's having a good time." Irene hopped down the stairs, craning her neck so she could get a good view of Leah and Benton's work hanging the garland. "It's fun meeting new people, too, like Paige. Her baby is such a peach."

"Poppy is pretty cute." Benton secured the garland on another hook.

"You like babies?" Irene's eyebrows wiggled. "Leah does, too. Whenever a patient's family visits and brings a baby, watch out. I'm surprised Leah didn't go into pediatrics. She'll be such a good mom."

Leah's chest and neck heated in a fierce blush. In a second her face would be as red as the bow in her hand. "Everyone likes babies, Irene."

"Not everyone. Benton, do you want kids?" Irene's innocent tone didn't fool Leah. Unfortunately, Irene pretended to be absorbed in the length of the garland loops and refused to meet Leah's pointed glare.

Benton didn't look up, either. "Someday, I hope."

"When you meet the right woman, of course. Unless you're dating someone already?"

Leah was tempted to leap over the banister and tell her friend to knock it off. Face hot as a pancake griddle, Leah jiggled the garland instead. "That drape looks good, Benton."

"Thanks. And um, no, Irene. I'm steadfastly single."

"Ooh, steadfast?"

Kellan and Phil returned to the foyer, sandwiches in hand. "Benton, do you want to eat before we do the lights on that house out back?"

"I do. Perfect timing. The garland is finished." Benton glanced at Leah. "I mean, unless you need me for something else right now?"

"Nope, I'm good." Grateful for the interruption to Irene's nosy and embarrassing line of questioning, Leah avoided eye contact with him by tweaking a bow.

"Coming, Irene?" Phil's tone was sweet. "There's a turkey cranberry, your favorite."

"I'll wait for Leah."

Leah fiddled with the bow until she could hear Phil's and Benton's voices mingling with the other men's in the kitchen. Then she marched downstairs, close enough to whisper to Irene. "What was that about, asking if he's single?"

"Not for me, Leah. I'm happy with Phil. I was asking for you."

"I caught that, yeah. And I'm sure he did, too." She bent to fuss with another bow. "This situation is awkward enough without people assuming there's anything romantic going on."

"He's so cute and sweet, though." Irene's voice rose. "You work well together, too. Just date him already. Get rid of your no-pastors dating rule once and for all."

"You don't date pastors, missy?" The familiar female voice of Maude Donalson was so loud, it echoed through the foyer.

Mortified, Leah stood up. Oh, no. Things went from bad to worse. Maude wasn't alone. Beside her was Benton, his face inscrutable before he said something about Maude offering to help and left.

He couldn't possibly be hurt, could he?

Leaving his half-eaten roast beef and horseradish sandwich in the kitchen, Benton went out back to open boxes of lights. The past few minutes had been rather uncomfortable, to say the least, what with Irene's questions, then seeing Maude nosing about the side of the house and then walking into something about a "no-pastor dating rule" of Leah's.

It wasn't like he had any intention of advancing his relationship with Leah past the gala. Why did it sting, then? It wasn't personal against him. Then again, it sort of was, if she had something against pastors. Which was odd, since her dad had been one.

The kitchen door shut behind him with a slap. Kellan and Tom bounded down the porch steps.

"Phil's still eating, but we're all done. What are you thinking for the outdoor lights?" Tom asked. "Are there enough to hang strands along the eaves, or are we just doing the porch?"

"We have enough to do the whole thing."

"Kellan and I can do this if you want to go back inside and finish your sandwich." Tom rubbed his stubbled jaw.

"Or if you want to help Leah with something." Kellan smirked.

Tom's hearty laugh was enough to put Benton off lunch entirely. "Not you guys, too."

"Who else is giving you a hard time about Leah?"

"Irene. Don't ask."

Kellan flicked a lock of blond hair from his brow. "Maude complained to Paige that you and Leah have a thing."

"There's no thing."

"Are you sure?"

"Of course, I'm sure. Just because we're spending time together on gala stuff doesn't mean there's anything going on."

Kellan had the grace to look abashed. "Well, Leah was wearing your scarf yesterday at the tree lot. The one we got you for your birthday last month."

Benton gritted his teeth. "She was cold."

Tom clapped him on the shoulder. "You're a good guy, Benton, but you know how women interpret things like that."

"Leah didn't interpret it that way at all. Trust me. She's not remotely interested."

Kellan frowned. "Sorry, dude."

"Don't be sorry. I'm not upset about it. Can we just hang the lights, please?"

"Sure thing." Tom gave Kellan a speaking look that Benton didn't miss, but at least they didn't bring it up again as they hung the lights. It didn't take long, with three of them tackling the job, and Phil joined them before they hung lights on the staff house. After setting up the light displays on the grass, they positioned a few solar-powered lights that looked like candy canes along the walkway to the staff house.

They were finishing up when Leah stepped out onto the front porch, cradling a screaming bundle with flailing fists. Despite the baby's distress, Leah's demeanor was calm as she gently bounced the baby.

"Uh-oh." Kellan rushed to the porch.

Benton's stomach clenched. "Is she okay?"

"Ready to go home." Leah handed the baby to Kellan. "Paige is gathering your stuff."

Faith exited the house, too, holding out the baby's diaper bag. "Tom, we should go, too. Your mom texted, and Logan's complaining of a sore throat."

"Sorry to leave before we're finished, guys." Tom held out his hands in an apologetic gesture.

"No, I think we're done. The inside is set, for the most part," Leah insisted, as they all returned inside the house. "My grandma is fatigued, anyway. Thanks for your help, everyone. We couldn't have done this without you."

"It was a blast." Paige met them in the foyer, carrying the baby's infant seat. "I can't wait to see how it looks at nighttime."

Maude wandered out from the parlor with a half-eaten cookie in hand. "If I'd have been invited today, I'd have brought home-baked cookies. Mine are much better."

Benton didn't care for the whine in her tone, but he knew Maude's words came from a place of loneliness. "You're a great baker, Maude, but we didn't want to put you to work today."

"That's right. You're a blue-ribbon gingerbread baker." Leah rapped her fingers on the banister. "We need gingerbread cookies for the gala, Maude. A lot of them. Are you available for hire?"

"You want my cookies?" Maude gaped. "Yes, yes, I am available."

What a brilliant idea. Leah was involving Maude and fulfilling a need at the same time—

"I don't like this," a shrill female voice insisted in the foyer.

Leah rushed past Maude, and Benton followed her. "Grandma, are you all right?"

Clare looked suspiciously at Leah before shoving the blanket to the ground. "Get it away from me."

"No need for it if you're warm enough, Grandma." As Leah bent to gather it, Clare swatted at her as if she were a fly. Not enough to cause pain, but Leah's feelings must be hurt.

Benton stepped up to the chair. "Clare?"

"It's okay," Leah interrupted. "She's either in pain or tired. Either way we should go back to CRV. Sorry to leave in such a rush."

"No, I need to go work on the parish hall."

"My son will be glad to hear that," Maude said.

He escorted Rowena to Leah's car, told everyone goodbye, and tidied up. This was not how he wanted to end the day, in a jumble of folks hurriedly leaving and Clare in distress. Pretty much everything on the to-do list had been accomplished, including polishing silver bowls for the hot chocolate station. They even had cookies taken care of. But the day felt… Unfinished. Strange.

He couldn't shake the feeling as he opened a paint can and started on the edges. He'd told Odell he wouldn't paint until Monday, but they'd finished earlier than expected at Hughes House and he had free time now. Within two hours, though, he cleaned off the brush, ready to call it a day. He needed dinner, a shower and a good night's sleep.

On the way, he drove back to Hughes House. The sun had set, and it would be a good idea to see if the timers he'd set up on the house lights worked how he wished.

He needn't have worried about any of that, because when he pulled up to Hughes House, the place was lit like a holiday wonderland. Scores of white lights framed each of the three stories' worth of windows and netted the shrubbery. Illumined by the glow, Leah stood on the circular drive, dressed in her thick coat and a beanie with a pom-pom on the top.

She shook her head when he got out of his car. "We can't stay away, can we?"

"I guess not." Benton joined her on the driveway, his words steaming in the cool evening air. "How's your grandma?"

"She seemed glad to be back in her room. She was sweet, in fact. I don't know what agitated her earlier, but the situation improved." Leah stared at the porch with unfocused eyes. "It can be tough, not knowing what's going on inside her sometimes."

Benton couldn't imagine. "You gave her a good day. She was happy."

"For a few hours, she was indeed." Leah tipped her head, making the pom-pom on her hat wobble. "Anyway, what are you doing here?"

"Testing the lights, but you beat me to it."

"It looks wonderful, doesn't it?"

"Thanks to our friends' help. I mean, Faith and Tom have shops. So does Kellan, and he and Paige must be exhausted with a newborn. Nice to meet Phil and Irene, too. She's your boss?"

"And my best friend. Speaking of Irene." Leah shoved her hands into her coat pockets. "I owe you an explanation for what you walked into earlier."

"No, you don't."

"I want to. My dad was a pastor," she reminded him.

"Was he called away a lot?"

"Of course. Pastors are like doctors, on call. I understood that and never minded it, even as a kid when he missed two of my birthdays. But it's more than that. Some parishioners were judgmental about how frugal our vacations were, what type of shoes we wore, how poorly my mom played piano. They saw everything we did and analyzed it, and it fell below their expectations. On top of that, when some girls bullied me, I stood up for myself, but was told by someone at church that I wasn't making a good impression on visitors. I was supposed to be a PK. Not Pastor's Kid. *Perfect* Kid."

"Yikes."

"Then my parents were killed in a car crash and no one reached out to us. When the cops came to tell us—Grandma was spending the weekend with us—all the neighbors stood out front of their houses and watched. No one came over. Including a family from church."

"That's terrible, Leah. Sometimes people don't know what the right thing to do is, but I can't imagine how abandoned you must have felt."

"It was devastating. But after that, once we lived with Grandma, I didn't feel like I lived in a fishbowl anymore."

"Not all people are like that. Not all churches are like that."

"I know. But I don't want to find out the hard way again. That's why I told Irene I didn't ever want to date a pastor."

"I understand. I'm single on purpose. Encumbered by stuff I can't quite shake."

"Parishioners' expectations?"

"Not how you're thinking." He deliberated for a few seconds. "Can I tell you about it over pizza?"

He expected her to say no, but she smiled. "If we order delivery from DeLuca's and eat here, we can enjoy the lights for a little longer."

"I'd like that."

It was ten days to the gala. Ten days until their partnership ended. But he wanted to confide in her. Felt he could trust her. And if they could part as friends when this gala was over, he'd be happy. Because having her as a friend meant never having to lose this relationship, and it was becoming more and more precious to him by the day.

Chapter Eight

An hour later, Benton stared at the remnants of their feast, two skinny pieces of pepperoni pizza in the box and a puddle of Italian dressing in the black plastic salad bowl. "We polished off the antipasto."

"We worked up an appetite today. You worked harder than me, though." Leah gestured at Benton's hands.

He hadn't realized they were flecked with paint. "I only did the edges around the doors, stuff like that. Do you approve of the color?"

"Off-white? It's basic, but basic is good for a parish hall."

"*Off-white?* Aren't you the woman who noted the monumental differences between maroon, berry and burgundy?" He pointed at a fleck. "I'll have you know it's *eggshell*."

"Looks more like water chestnut," she teased. "No church members are willing to help?"

"I'm not asking them. Folks are busy this time of year."

"But your congregation knows you're doing this?"

"The elder board does. Odell, Maude's son, is the one

who talked to me about doing things as a cost-saving measure." Just thinking about Odell's texts pushing for faster results made him grimace. "I agreed to it, so I shouldn't burden anyone else."

"I can help. I'm a decent painter and a parish hall is a lot of wall to cover for one person."

"No, I'm good."

"You asked people to help us decorate Hughes House. Why not ask for help with the parish hall, too?"

"Because the gala is for the community, but the parish hall is my job. My responsibility."

She shook her head at him. "Come on, let's go look at the Christmas tree."

"There's not anywhere to sit in the foyer." He followed her, carrying their paper plates and the antipasto container. She stuck the pizza box into the humming retro refrigerator, and he dumped their plates into the trash and rinsed out the salad bowl for recycling.

"Let's sit on the stairs." She sounded excited at the prospect. "When I was little I always wanted to sit on the stairs and look down at a Christmas tree, but we always lived in one-story houses."

"Me, too."

"Let's do it then. And I know you said you wanted to talk about your dating life over pizza, but we got busy talking about other things. It's okay, too. We don't have to talk about dating. We can talk about the gala. Or nothing at all, if you want."

"That sounds...amazing." Sitting in companionable silence with her, enjoying the tree, would be a relaxing end to this day. "But since the whole thing came up, I want to tell you. Especially since the mayor keeps making pointed comments."

"The mayor? I thought you were going to say Maude, trying to pair you off." Leah's eyes narrowed. "You mean about us conning Rowena out of this house?"

"She's talking to me, not you." At her confused look, he tipped his head toward the kitchen door. "Come on. Stairs first."

They climbed almost to the landing at the second floor, sitting side by side on a cold wood step, the tree and the other decorations in the foyer in full view below them. One of Paige's tabletop decorations took pride of place on the marble table, holding the spot until the gingerbread house was ready. "Looks good for the gala, doesn't it."

"It does." He ran a hand through his hair. "I told you I'd never been to a Gingerbread Gala, and that's true. But this won't be the first year I was here, at this house, on the night of December twenty-first. Nineteen years ago, I crashed a car into Rowena's Cadillac, which she'd parked out on the street."

Leah's jaw went slack. "Oh, no, were you hurt?"

"No. Just her car."

"Still, that must've been scary. Especially when you were a young driver. You must have just received your license."

"I didn't have a license at all. I'd just turned fourteen."

"You drove without a license? Did you even know how to drive a car?"

"Nope. It was winter vacation, no school in the morning, and my older brother, Jarod, went to a friend's house about a block down the street from here. Turned out the parents were at the Gingerbread Gala, and the kids took advantage of their absence by drinking. I got a phone call from the kid's little sister, panicking because Jarod was planning to drive home and she thought our dad should come get him, instead. But Dad was passed out. He'd been drinking, too. I was too ashamed and afraid to ask some other adult. Not that I knew who to ask, anyway, so I ran through record rainfall to the kids' house so I could save the day and drive Jarod home."

"That sounds like such a traumatic experience."

"It was, and it was the wrong thing to do. I had no clue what I was doing, but how hard could it be, right?" He threw up his hands.

"It may have been wrong—"

"And illegal."

She chewed her lip. "Okay, yes, but you did it so your brother didn't drive drunk."

"I started out doing great, too. I drove Jarod's '66 Mustang a whole block before I hydroplaned into Rowena's car."

She reached for his arm. "You could've been killed. I'm so glad—" Her cheeks flushed and she pulled back as if she'd done the wrong thing, touching his sleeve so softly he didn't even feel the fabric of his sweat-shirt move.

"Yeah, me, too. Glad no one got hurt."

She clutched her hands in her lap. "That's why Mayor Hughes called us criminals."

"That's why she called *me* one, yes. She was there that night, one of a handful of people who ran outside once they heard the crash. But Jarod—well, here's the thing. Jarod ran away. So what the mayor saw, what everyone but Rowena saw, was me alone with the crashed car. And I didn't correct their impressions that I'd taken my brother's car for a joyride."

"Why not?"

"I was trying to protect him. Still am, I guess. At the time, I didn't want Jarod to get into worse trouble with my dad. We moved away not long afterward, and since then, I've felt the part about him drinking isn't my secret to tell. Or that he has a problem with alcohol abuse to this day." He glanced at her. "Not even Kellan knows about Jarod's involvement."

She licked her lips. "But Rowena knew?"

"She saw Jarod run off, but she followed my lead and kept it to herself. She was nothing but kind, then and now. Never held it against me. The bottom line, though, is the crash isn't a secret. The elder board at church knows."

"I'm so sorry, Benton."

He stretched out his legs and leaned back against the stair behind him. "I was scared and clueless. Nowadays, there are options. Uber or Lyft or a taxi. But the kids in Good Shepherd's youth group also know I'm available 24-7 to drive someone home. They also know I'm not okay with sin and I'm not going to turn a blind eye to bad choices, but if one of my kids ends up in a situation they don't know how to get out of? If a friend or relative is about to get behind the wheel? I want to make sure they're safe, first and foremost. Then we'll have a talk about it."

"I wish you'd had someone like you back then."

"I do, too. My mom took us to church before she died. I knew she loved God because she had that sampler of the Scripture verse. Not sure where it is now, but I know, had she lived, things would've been different. Anyway, my envy of kids with involved parents and pastors is what first got me into church when I went to college. That's how I met God. How He grabbed ahold of my life. All I wanted was to follow Him, but then I felt called to be a pastor. It didn't seem right. I couldn't believe He would use someone like me in ministry."

"He uses everyone, silly." She stretched out her legs, too. "This is just how He's using you."

"I'm a failure when it comes to ministering to my family, though. I told you about my dad. He says he's off the bottle but wants money all the time."

"What about your brother? How's Jarod now?"

"He says he's doing all right." For now.

"Good. I'll pray for him. And your dad."

"Thanks. Anyway, that's the long and short of it. I have a family with a big problem, and to some people, like the mayor, that makes me a not-good pastor."

"That's ridiculous."

"She's not the only one. I did have a girlfriend for a while, at my last church. Not a parishioner, of course, but someone I met at the city's ecumenical prayer gathering. Katie. I thought, well, it doesn't matter. But when it came time to meet my dad, he showed up drunk, and she set me straight. If I can't be a good son and brother, and help them lean on Jesus for their sobriety, maybe I'm not the best pastor I could be. And I definitely shouldn't bring a woman into it."

"I don't—" Leah stared at the tree. "I'm sorry, but you can't control other people's choices."

"That doesn't mean Katie was wrong. I have a duty to help my family." He nudged her with his shoulder. "You know pastors' lives are complicated. That's why you're not going to date one."

"I'm glad I'm friends with one, though." Her eyes

were dark liquid in the light of the tree. "I'm glad you shared with me."

"I haven't known you long, Leah, but I trust you."

"I trust you, too. And I don't trust many people." Facing him, she was close enough for him to catch the faint dusting of freckles on her nose. Close enough to feel like he shouldn't stare into her eyes, so his gaze dropped to her lips. Then it swiftly rose to her eyes again because looking at her lips made him think of kissing her.

Kissing Leah? No way. A hundred times no. But right now, after telling her about his past and her listening, supporting, caring? Sitting on the steps, in the sweet glow of the Christmas tree lights, inches from her beautiful face?

It was easy to forget his decision not to date. And that he was the one type of man she didn't want to be involved with, ever.

He hopped to his feet. "It's getting late. Sundays are early for me."

"Oh, of course. I need to get to Ralph, anyway."

Their regular lives waited, lives that would still be there long after the gala. This was an anomaly. A temporary blip in both of their lives.

But that night, he couldn't shake the feeling that something had changed. He never should have thought of kissing her.

Three days later, Leah wondered if she was making a mistake.

Since she and Benton shared pizza and honest conversation at Hughes House on Saturday night, their relationship had shifted. They hadn't worked together— they had no plans to until they assembled the gingerbread house the following weekend—but they texted each day. Not about the gala, either.

He asked about her church service on Sunday and how her grandma fared, and she shared tidbits about Sunday's sermon and admitted Grandma seemed restless. He told her he'd bought a skinny tree from Taylor's and reminded her they had plans to decorate it after the gala. She inquired about his Sunday and his progress in the parish hall, and he told her how he researched sermons and sent cell phone pictures of eggshell-colored paint. She sent pictures of Ralph wearing a festive tartan coat to keep him warm on their walk. They shared jokes and encouragement.

Chitchat between friends, nothing more. That's how the topic of tonight's choir concert at Good Shepherd Church had come up. Benton hadn't invited her so much as mentioned it, adding it was open to the community. A week ago, she wouldn't have dared attending, fearing that one of his parishioners, like Maude, might get the wrong impression about their relationship if she showed up in his church.

Since Saturday, though, Leah wasn't worried about it anymore. She and Benton were friends. She wanted to support him. If she could listen to Christmas music while doing it, so much the better. Regardless of what anyone thought about them being together so much, she and Benton were on the same page. He knew about her no-pastor rule, and it wasn't like he wanted to date her, either.

However, now that she'd arrived at Good Shepherd with Irene and Rowena, her stomach felt like a ball of nerves. Breathing deeply, she prayed for peace.

Benton slipped through the crowd, his smile dazzling. "You all came. Thanks, ladies."

"I'm excited. For the music, I mean." Self-conscious, Leah shoved a lank of hair behind her ear. She wore it down tonight, the loose waves from her curling iron trailing down her back.

"Absolutely." His gaze followed the motion of her hand.

"Phil had a commitment, but he's sorry to miss it." Irene gestured at the aged stained-glass windows, lit up from the outside to make them sparkle for those inside tonight. "It's so pretty in here."

"It's even prettier inside." Rowena squeezed Benton's arm. "We'd better get seats while we can. Packed house, I think."

"I've got to excuse myself, too. See you later?" Benton's question was for them all, but his gaze didn't leave Leah's.

"Of course." She watched him greet another group before entering the sanctuary. In style, it was a lot like the church Leah's dad had pastored. Not tiny, but cozy, and it was dressed up for the season with pine boughs and potted poinsettias. A strange sensation hit Leah in the chest. Not grief, which she expected, but lightness, as if those associations unleashed a golden warmth through her veins. Thinking of her parents, she squeezed into the pew between Rowena and Irene, taking in the hum of chatter and the air of expectancy in the room.

Irene divested her houndstooth coat, using the opportunity to lean into Leah. "Benton seems awfully glad you're here."

"And that you're here, too."

Irene executed one perfectly arched brow of disbelief.

Thankfully, someone chose that moment to pat her shoulder from behind. Leah twisted around, glad to see her favorite volunteer on Grandma's ward. "Marigold. How are you?"

"Feeling festive," Marigold said in her high-pitched voice. She sounded a little like a Christmas elf. "You'll be glad to know I bought my ticket to the Gingerbread Gala."

"Thank you. I hope you enjoy it."

"I will. You and our pastor are working hard on it together, I hear?"

There was something fishy in Marigold's tone. Benton had mentioned Marigold played matchmaker for Kellan and Paige. Was she thinking of doing the same here?

She and Maude would be at odds, then. Leah had best disabuse Marigold of any romantic notions now. "Not just us. Saturday, a whole crew helped."

The lights dimmed and the choir entered the sanctuary then, so Leah smiled at Marigold and turned around in her seat. Irene nudged her in the ribs. "I'm not the only one seeing potential between you and the pastor."

Leah rolled her eyes at Irene before focusing on the choir. Before the first song ended, she'd become engrossed in the beautiful music. Her heart and mind both engaged in the pieces, and she began to consider the great gifts of Christmas, especially Jesus, coming as a baby in Bethlehem.

The time passed swiftly, and Leah was almost shocked when Benton rose from one of the front pews and stood in front of the choir. He looked like he belonged there, speaking with confidence as he thanked the choir, director and organist for the gifts of their hard work. Then, after offering a brief message on the meaning of Christmas, he thanked the guests for coming.

"Thank you for bringing me." Rowena looped her arm through Leah's as they made their way down the center aisle. "This was fun."

"It was," Irene agreed. "Don't forget, we have to see Benton before we go. You promised, Leah."

Leah felt herself almost dragged into the church's entry area, Rowena on one side, Irene on the other. "I'd hate to bother him if he's busy."

Rowena tipped her head in Benton's direction. "There he is. Not busy at all."

He was indeed busy, conversing with three teenagers. Leah hated to interrupt that, but the kids moved off and Irene closed the gap before someone else could command Benton's attention. "Spectacular concert, and the church was beautiful."

"And a powerful message, too." Leah met Benton's smiling gaze.

"I couldn't pass up an opportunity to share the Gospel. But when it comes to the music, I might be biased, but I think the choir and musicians are outstanding. One of the women's groups gets all the credit for the boughs and flowers, though." He held his hands up. "I don't even water the potted poinsettias in the sanctuary. I'm afraid I'd kill them."

Rowena laughed. "Surely your thumb isn't that brown. As a matter of fact, it's speckled yellowish."

Splotches of eggshell paint had dried on his hand. With a sheepish smile, he rubbed the flecks. "A souvenir from the parish hall."

"Is it almost done?" a nasal masculine voice said

from behind Leah. She startled to realize a tall, graying man stood in her personal space. As she inched away, he pushed into the spot where she'd been standing. "I'd like to see for myself, but the parish hall is locked."

Maybe it was Leah's imagination, but the light in Benton's eyes seemed to dim. His smile stayed constant, though. "Good evening, Odell. Yes, it was decided the parish hall should be off-limits until the work is finished. We wouldn't want anyone tripping on the uneven flooring, but I'd be happy to show you if you can wait a few minutes."

Ah, Odell. So this was the guy who was so concerned with the parish hall.

"Talking about the gala?" Maude appeared from nowhere, clutching both Odell's and Benton's arms.

"No, Mother, the parish hall." Odell's clipped tone made his frustration clear. "I'm growing increasingly concerned that it won't be finished in time for the pageant."

Rowena eyed Odell. "We have a beautiful sanctuary to host the pageant in, you know."

"It's not traditional." Odell's thin brows lowered over his eyes. "The pageant has been held in the parish hall since the stage's construction over fifty years ago—"

"There's time for Pastor Benton to tidy the parish hall after the gala. You know I'm baking the gingerbread people for it." Maude's chest puffed out with pride.

"No one cares about that right now, Mother," Odell barked. "The parish hall is the pastor's priority. It's his job, not that silly gala."

Oh, dear. Benton hadn't exaggerated Odell's impatience about the parish hall. Poor Maude's face crumpled like she was about to cry.

Benton patted her shoulder. "We're all excited for the gingerbread cookies, Maude. And as for the parish hall, Odell, give me a minute and we can head over."

Before he finished speaking, a man with Benton's eyes and build approached him from behind, clamping his shoulders in a firm grip. "Surprise."

Benton's eyes widened and he spun around. Then he enveloped the man in a hug. "Jarod."

"You weren't at your house, so I knew you had to be here. I missed the fun, eh?"

This was the brother she'd heard about, huh? He wasn't quite as handsome as Benton, but he was well-dressed and charming. Each member of their group got a firm handshake and winsome smile as Benton introduced them.

"Nice to meet all you good folks."

"What brings you to town?" Benton's smile looked apprehensive.

Jarod punched his shoulder. "Can't I visit my brother for Christmas?"

Christmas wasn't for another ten days, but maybe Jarod was here because he wanted a better relationship with his younger brother. Maybe he would help Benton talk to their dad as a united front, and even go to church.

Whatever his reason for surprising Benton tonight, God might have something big in mind. Leah prayed it meant Benton's family would come together on a more solid foundation. It would bring Benton some healing and peace, but also, he'd said he wouldn't consider having a family of his own until his family of origin was in better shape.

He'd be free to love and be loved.

Certainly, there'd be a wonderful woman for him.

Maybe no one of Maude's choosing, but perhaps someone else in town. Someone who wanted to be a pastor's wife.

Leah felt happy for him, even though right now Odell glared at him and his brother commanded all the attention. Benton deserved a happy life.

Then why did the thought of him eventually getting married make her feel so sad?

Chapter Nine

"Leah, dear, I must ask. Were you Benton's date for the choir concert the other night?" Marigold's wide eyes seemed innocent enough, considering how loaded her question was.

Leah and Marigold sat by Grandma's bedside while she dozed on Friday afternoon. As peaceful as Grandma looked now, one would never have guessed she was so agitated most of the afternoon. Leah had taken the afternoon off to sit with her. "No, Marigold. I wasn't."

"Too bad. You're just the type of sweetheart we've been praying for when it comes to our beloved pastor getting paired off." Marigold frowned, as if disappointed. "Forgive me if I embarrassed you. I can be a bit nosy at times. My grandchildren call it meddling, but I call it love. I played matchmaker for Kellan and Paige." Her face the picture of innocence, Marigold fiddled with the volunteer badge hanging from a bright blue lanyard around her neck.

Marigold's pushing, or meddling or whatever she wanted to call it, put her at odds with Maude—and it wouldn't work with Leah and Benton. "I'm leaving town soon. Taking Grandma to a different facility in the San Francisco area that offers more programs for patients like Grandma. Music therapy, that sort of thing."

Leah half expected an argument, but Marigold reached to squeeze her hand. "You and Clare will both be missed around here."

"Thank you for all you do, visiting folks on the ward."

"It's my pleasure. I love helping the nurses and sitting with folks. We talk about the good old days. Your grandma, too."

"Oh, yeah?"

"Not every time, of course, but sometimes, we have the nicest conversations about her high school days. Football championships, cherry sodas, happy times." Marigold's sigh sounded content. "We sing, too."

"She sang on Saturday. She knew all the words to a dozen Christmas carols. She even ate a few cookies, but today, she's not interested in her food."

Lord, please may Hughes House sell quickly so that I can give Grandma a better quality of life. One filled with music.

"And what about you, dear? Are you enjoying the holiday season, too?"

Leah had to laugh. "I'm in the thick of it for the gala, that's for sure."

"I saw the article on the gala in the county newspaper today."

What article? Leah hadn't seen today's edition. "I put in ads, but I don't know anything about an article. I'll have to pick up a copy. Did they include information about how to get tickets?"

"No, it wasn't that type of article. More about the

Gingerbread Galas of the past, but it mentions Rowena is giving you the house in exchange for you throwing the gala. I don't know where they got that sort of information."

"Indeed." Leah hadn't told anyone but Irene. Benton may have told a few friends, but they didn't seem the type to go to a newspaper about it. The mayor knew about Rowena's gift, though, and she might have talked to a reporter.

Leah couldn't worry about it. "Hopefully, the exposure causes people to buy tickets. I can't believe the party is in a few days. Benton and I have to put together the gingerbread house this evening."

"Have to? I'd say you *get* to. What a fun date." Marigold giggled. "Not a date, sorry."

Leah gently brushed a tendril of Grandma's pale frizz from her forehead. "After the day Grandma had, maybe I should stay. I'll see if Benton can reschedule with me."

"Why put it off, dear? She's sleeping. And if she wakes, she's safe. And while I never knew Clare particularly well, I do know she wouldn't want you here when you could be decorating a gingerbread house with a handsome young man. Even if it's not a date."

Marigold had a point. On top of that, Leah had baked the gingerbread pieces last night. They were ready to assemble and decorate, and this had been the best hole in both her and Benton's schedules. He'd been busy with church stuff, and his brother was in town, now, too. And Grandma was indeed sleeping...

Go have fun. Leah wasn't sure where that memory of her grandma came from. A high school dance, maybe? One of Leah's younger brothers got the flu and Leah felt obligated to stay home to care for him, even though he wasn't that sick and Grandma was more than capable of tending him. Leah had felt guilty anyway, and Grandma had practically shooed her out the door.

Her time with Benton—as a friend, of course—was running short. After the gala, they wouldn't have an excuse to hang out, and Leah couldn't deny he was… Special. No, that sounded too romantic. A good friend, someone in whom she could confide and who confided in her. A person who had earned her trust in a way few others had. She'd leave the definition of their relationship right there.

Leah checked her watch. "All right. I'd like to eat a quick dinner and change out of my scrubs before I meet Benton at Hughes House."

"I'll stay with Clare a little longer. Enjoy the gingerbread, dear." Marigold waved both hands at her as if Leah was a fly she tried to shoo out the door.

Leah kissed Grandma's forehead and left.

So far, Leah's evening had been anything but fun.

She'd gone home to change and eat, but Ralph was so clingy and whiny, she decided he needed her company. Bundling up his favorite blanket and some dog treats, she'd brought him along to Hughes House. Once she'd arrived, arms laden with gingerbread, she'd gone to use the restroom and almost slipped on a puddle spilling from beneath the powder room floor.

Grumbling, she'd shut off the water valve and texted Benton, who was running late at a hospital visit, but he said he'd be there as soon as possible, and he'd handle the plumbing himself.

Hopefully, the evening would improve from there.

Ralph explored while she laid out the gingerbread pieces on the kitchen table, and just as she finished, she heard the front door creak open. With a clipped bark, Ralph bolted toward the foyer.

"Hey, boy. I didn't know you'd be here but I'm glad to see you."

Leah entered the foyer to the charming sight of Benton, surrounded by grocery bags, kneeling on the black-and-white tile floor, rubbing Ralph behind the ears. Ralph shifted his weight between his feet, switching back and forth every second or so.

"I call that his tap dance." Leah leaned against the wall. "Because of the sound his claws make."

"Are you tap-dancing, boy?" Benton allowed Ralph to sniff his nose before picking up the grocery bags he'd set down.

"I hope you don't mind that I brought him. He seemed lonely." Benton and Ralph followed her back to the kitchen.

"Not at all." He set the bags on the Formica counter. "Let's look at that leak."

Maybe she'd misunderstood his intention to fix it, though, because he didn't carry a toolbox. "Did you call a plumber?"

"No, I can handle it, but Kellan borrowed my tools and I'm going to need my pipe wrenches. Since I was running behind due to a hospital visit, he said he'd run it over here to save me time."

She and Ralph followed him down the hall. Stepping over the towels she'd laid down to mop the mess, he turned the water valve on, lay on his back under the sink, and after a few seconds asked Leah to turn on the faucet. "Okay, I see where the water's coming from.

You can turn it off." He reemerged. "Easy fix, once I have the tools."

"That's good, because I need you tonight." Leah caught herself. "I mean, I'm glad you can help with the gingerbread house."

She spun on her heel and returned to the kitchen, kicking herself. For someone who didn't want to date a pastor, she was sure blurting out things that made it sound like she'd changed her mind.

Benton and Ralph followed her back to the kitchen. "Is something wrong?"

"No. I mean, it's been a long day with Grandma. Oh, and Marigold told me there's an article about the gala in the county newspaper. I haven't had a chance to look at it yet, but it includes the news that Rowena is giving Hughes House to us. That's private, I thought. I mean, I told Irene, but that's not the same as telling a newspaper."

"I'm sure my friends didn't share it, either. My guess is Mayor Hughes said something, but we can't let it bother us."

"We didn't do anything wrong, and Rowena's of sound mind. This is legal. The lawyer said so."

"Exactly. By the way, it smells amazing in here. Look at all your hard work."

Thankful he didn't seem to notice her flub, she joined him at the table to examine the gingerbread pieces— slabs which would become walls, a roof, and the chimneys. She'd mixed the dough, rich in cinnamon, nutmeg and, of course, ginger, then rolled and cut it into shapes according to Benton's measurements and baked them at home. "Let's just hope the house stays up." She laughed self-deprecatingly.

"It will, don't worry. Hey, what's all this?" He gestured to a stretch of counter by the kitchen sink, where she'd left gallon-sized baggies of food coloring, shredded wheat cereal and coconut flakes.

"Grass and bushes, in theory."

"That's a great idea. Why do you sound down about it?"

"The color's wrong."

"Looks green to me."

"My first attempt was too pastel, like butter mints, so I added more green food coloring, and now it's too forest-y."

"You and your color names." His teasing eyes sparkled, and she'd never seen his dimples so deep.

She shook her head as if his lack of skill differentiating hues was a great tragedy. "Someday you'll need to match a tie to a shirt or something and believe me, you won't want butter mint when the situation calls for forest. Tease me all you want, but you know I'm right."

"I do, but teasing you is too fun to pass up."

It was? *Oh, stop it. He's being nice.* Her cheeks warming from an unwelcome blush, she jumped out of her skin when Ralph barked. A second later, the doorbell rang with its loud, old-fashioned *ding-dong* notes. "That must be Kellan."

"I'll let him in."

While Benton went to the door, Leah laid out Ralph's blanket and offered him a biscuit. "Ralphie, I'm acting like a dummy. Tell me to stop it."

He just stared at her with sympathetic eyes.

"Hey, Leah," Kellan called.

She shouted a greeting, then unpacked her mixing bowls of royal icing while the guys talked plumbing, metal pipes and corrosion in old houses. Everything in the kitchen was set up to construct the house when they entered the kitchen.

"My plumber's putty dried out." Benton shook his head. "I have to run out to the hardware store. Sorry to leave you with this, Leah."

"I'll go," Kellan offered. "You're needed here, and it's the least I can do, seeing as how I kept your tools too long."

"Hardly," Benton said.

Leah chewed her lip. "I hate taking you away from Paige and Poppy."

"Paige's great-aunt is visiting tonight, so they're in good company. Besides, you guys have enough to worry about. I'll be back in a few." Waving, he left the kitchen, and, in a few seconds, the front door creaked open and shut with a *thunk*.

"All right, then." Benton rubbed his hands. "One gingerbread house, coming up. But since we were talking about green things, I should warn you I tried to find some sort of green candy for the shutters. Four stores and I couldn't find anything that looked right, so I ended up online. I remembered you saying something about wafer cookies being the right size, but this was the best I could do. They're not the right shade of green. I'm sorry." He pulled a cardboard package from one of the paper bags. It was emblazoned with Japanese characters and pictures of green rectangles.

"Matcha green tea wafer cookies?" She read the English translation and opened the package to look at them.

"They're not right. I can hear it in your voice."

"If it sounds off, it's because they're perfect." He'd

worked far harder and longer to find suitable candy shutters than he had time for, busy as he was. That right there made them a precious gift. "They're the right size and everything." And if the shade of green was a shade or two lighter than the shutters of Hughes House? She could not have cared less. "What else did you bring?"

"Gummy circles for wreaths, skinny strings of red licorice to make bows," he narrated as he unpacked. "Cereal for the roof. Peppermint sticks for the porch columns. Truffles and button candies that might come in handy, and if not, we get to eat them all, and look at these cool green rock candies. If we cut off the stick handles, they're like trees."

She clapped her hands. "They'll be great for the little cypresses."

He seemed pleased by her approval. "Last but not least, I thought we could cut this up to make the bricks." The plastic tub he pulled out contained sour cherry candy belts. "It might be time consuming, though."

"Cutting them is less work than what I'd planned to do, which was using icing to look like mortar. I love how the dusted sugar on top of these belts makes them look textured. Even a little snowy. What a great find."

"I can't take credit." Benton chuckled. "One of the middle schoolers brought some to youth group a few weeks ago, and the kids' mouths were redder than red. Whatever color that is."

"You're hopeless with hues," she teased. "Scarlet? Crimson?"

"Red works."

"Maybe it would be easier to glue them on with icing before we put the house together. Except—"

"Except what?"

"I just read online that the assembled house should sit for two or three hours before it gets fully decorated. We'd have to wait to put on the wreaths and roof and shutters."

"We can make the wreaths and do the candy bushes and stuff while it dries, then."

"If you're busy, though, it's okay. You've got a parishioner in the hospital."

"No," he answered, so quickly Leah's breath caught. "I'm not leaving you. This is a partnership, right?"

His eyes were dark and rich as sipping chocolate, and she found herself drowning in their depths. Oh, boy. She swallowed hard. "Right."

Benton pulled out a kitchen chair. "So, where do we start?"

Cutting the belts in pieces went quickly once they formed a system. Then they dotted icing on the back of each "brick" and glued them in the typical bond pattern of the brick walls of Hughes House, the quiet punctuated by Ralph chewing the biscuit or scratching.

The front door opened. "Honey, I'm home," Kellan yelled like Ricky Ricardo.

"Got the putty?" Leah asked.

"Yup." Kellan entered the kitchen and eyed the house. "Looking good."

Benton stood up, reaching for the putty. "Thanks, brother."

"No, I'll patch it. You've got better things to do. In fact, I'm going to double-check all the sinks in the house while I'm here. I'd hate for you guys to walk into another plumbing issue on Tuesday."

"Wow, Kellan, thanks," Leah said. Benton clapped him on the shoulder, then rejoined her at the table. When almost all the pieces of candy belt were in place, Leah glanced at their diminished bowl of royal icing. "I'm glad I made extra. I had no clue how much we needed."

"Are we ready to put the walls together, then?"

"I think so." Leah reached for a cardboard base she'd wrapped in foil to use as a foundation. Earlier, she'd marked where the walls should go so there'd be enough room for a candy "yard." Benton's candy "trees" would make a perfect addition to her attempts at making "bushes" out of wheat pillows.

Benton applied the perfect amount of icing to the front wall and gently placed it on the base. "This is a lot easier to use than that frosting tube at the rec center. Should we glue a side wall on at the same time?"

"Sure." As she frosted it, a drip of icing from Benton's wall splattered on the foil. He swiped it with his forefinger and licked it. "Tastes better than the stuff from the rec center, too."

She gently set the side wall at a ninety-degree angle to his front wall. "Isn't it naughty to nibble on gingerbread houses?"

"At the gala, sure, but right now, someone has to taste-test it for accuracy."

"Icing accuracy. That's a thing?"

"Haven't you heard of the Gingerbread Police? Supersecret organization that ensures all gingerbread houses are made from 100 percent candy goodness?"

Leah made a point of looking at Ralph. "Can you believe what you're hearing, Ralphie? Me, neither—oh, this is sliding." She'd lessened her hold on the wall and it started to slip down on the foil.

"We need more icing on the base, maybe."

But it didn't help. Things just got messier looking,

coating their fingers, and unlike the candy bricks, the walls didn't want to stay in place. Leah had never expected their house to look professional, much less great, but she had assumed the walls would stay up on their own.

"More icing, maybe?" Benton didn't sound as frustrated as Leah felt.

"I don't think that's it. Too much icing is as problematic as too little." Frustration tightened her throat, but she'd determined to pray more when she felt overwhelmed, so she shut her eyes for a second. *Thank You, God, that so far none of the gingerbread has broken.* If it did, she'd have to bake more gingerbread and they'd have to start over, and time was something they did not have. *Please show us how to hold the walls together.*

They needed better glue.

That was it. Leah shoved back her chair so hard Ralph lifted his head.

Benton gaped. "Where are you going?"

"To the parlor. Like you said, no one's going to eat it." She didn't turn around. "I need my craft bag. Time for the glue gun."

Within fifteen minutes the house was assembled, thanks to the glue gun, warm in Benton's hand. While Leah iced over the glue holding the walls together—to complete the look, she'd said—he affixed the chimney to the roof. *Steady, steady, there.*

Not too shabby if he did say so himself. "I'm glad you left the glue gun here. This is slick."

"I thought I might need it, if a bow fell off a wreath or something."

"Is it cheating to use glue on a gingerbread house?"

"Maybe if we were in a contest." Leah shrugged. "For this? I don't know, but I won't tell if you don't."

"Ralph's not telling, are you, boy?" Benton smiled at the dog, who rested on his blanket.

Ralph blinked and lowered his head to rest on his paws.

Leah laughed. "He's a good secret keeper."

"How old is he?"

"A young man in dog terms. He's four. We've been together two years. He belonged to a woman who came to CRV and couldn't keep him. How could I say no to that face?" Leah reached for the box of cereal. "Since we used a glue gun on the walls, I don't think we need to wait a full two hours to start decorating. Want to do the roof while I make wreaths?"

He'd much prefer gluing cereal to tying miniature bows out of red licorice. "Sure."

"We'll be finished a lot faster than I expected. You'll have some time tonight to visit with your brother. How's it going, by the way?" She popped a piece of cereal into her mouth.

"To be honest, we haven't seen a lot of each other. He's seen some old friends, but I've been busy anyway. Some things came up at church." In addition to the toy drive, two parishioners had gone to the hospital, a couple needed marriage counseling and Jan, the office manager, caught the flu. But his brother had told him one thing, though. "He's not here for Christmas. He lost his job."

"I'm sorry about that. Unemployment is rough." She deftly folded the red candy into a tiny bow. "I don't mean to pry, but are you concerned it's alcohol related?"

It was a sign of their honesty with one another that

she asked, and he appreciated that he could be real with her. He'd been open with friends like Kellan to a point, but not quite like this. Maybe it was because Leah wasn't a member of his church, but it probably had more to do with their choice to be frank with one another and her vulnerability with him. He could trust her, and it warmed him to the core.

"He said he's not drinking, but I never quite believe my dad or my brother when they say that. That's part of the issue in our relationship. I don't really trust them. I want to. I pray to." He glued almost a whole row of cereal shingles before she spoke again.

"We're all shaped by our past experiences. Like it or not, they affect who we become."

"I don't want it to be who I am, though. I want my family to be healed, no matter what patterns have been set."

She used the glue gun to fix the little bow to a green gummy wreath. "I get that. Growing up the subject of speculation and gossip by a few people in our church body made me sensitive to being talked about. I know that's not healthy, nor is it forgiving of me. I guess I've been looking at it wrong. Who I became rather than who I can be."

"The key is knowing we're not finished yet. God is accomplishing change in us. Probably will keep on doing so, too, until he takes us home. God doesn't want us stuck in pits of unforgiveness or resentment, even if we feel we're entitled to it."

Leah smiled. "Thank you, Benton. You're a good pastor."

"I'm not your pastor, Leah. I'm your friend." One

he didn't want to lose when she moved away with her grandma.

She stared at him, her breathing shaky sounding. "I'm glad for that."

At once he was aware of the stillness in the room, the quiet pierced by Ralph's snuffled snores, Kellan's footsteps upstairs and the refrigerator's noisy hum.

Again, he felt the urge to bridge the gap between them and kiss her. Or say something to act on the magnetic pull he felt toward her.

He hopped to his feet. "Let's see how those matcha cookies work as shutters." Grabbing the box on the counter, he shut his eyes. *Lord, help me. I don't want to be attracted to Leah.*

Kellan stomped down the stairs. "I'm done and the plumbing looks fine," he called as he walked in the room, "but I found something you ought to see before the house goes on the market."

Benton's stomach sank. "Big trouble?"

"Looks like there was a leak at some point in the main bedroom wall."

"Ugh. I'll keep on with the shutters, while you check it out," Leah said.

"How bad?" Benton followed Kellan up the grand staircase.

"It's dry, but I just happened to notice a lumpy spot." Leading the way to the main bedroom, he showed Benton a patch of wall the size of his hand. "It wouldn't hurt to have a professional come in."

Benton ran his hand over the wallpaper. "You're right. One more thing for the task list."

"By the way, sorry to interrupt you and Leah." Kellan wiggled his brows.

"I'm glad you're here tonight, brother. I'm—I've got feelings for Leah and I wish I didn't."

"Because she's not interested, you said?" Kellan shook his head. "I don't know, man. I could hear you down in the kitchen, laughing and talking."

"Nope. Trust me. And it's a good thing she's not, because I'm not in any position to—well, I'm single for a reason."

"Which I don't quite get."

Benton rubbed his face with both hands. "It's complicated."

"Can't be any more complicated than my story when Paige came to town. God worked through it, and He is more than capable of working out whatever's bugging you." Kellan folded his arms. "You don't have to tell me anything, but I'm here if you need to talk. Even if our relationship is supposed to be the other way around, you're my friend, Benton."

"Thanks. For everything." Benton clapped his shoulder before tipping his head at the door. "I'll let you get back to your family now."

Before flicking off the light switch, Kellan's glance caught on the sampler hanging on the wall, the one so similar to the one his mother had made. *God is my strength and my song.*

He needed to focus on God, rely on God for his strength. Stop thinking of Leah as anything more than a friend.

When they returned to the kitchen, Leah had folded Ralph's blanket and packed up her things. "Is it bad?"

Oh, yeah, the leak. "No, it's old, but Kellan's right. It needs to be taken care of before the house sells. What's all this? You're heading home?"

"It's been a long day for both of us, so I thought we should all go out together. I can finish the gingerbread house tomorrow."

"I don't want to leave it on your plate, Leah."

"There's not much left. I've got it. You spend time with your brother." She hoisted her purse over her shoulder. "Thanks for the help, Kellan."

"No problem." Kellan's smile didn't hide the fact that his brain was busy processing the conversation he and Benton had upstairs. Couldn't he see that Leah wasn't interested in being more than friends? If she had feelings for him, surely she'd want to stay and finish the house with him—no. It wasn't worth thinking about. This was all on him.

If he ended up with a broken heart, he had no one to blame but himself.

Chapter Ten

"I can't believe you." Irene shook her head at Leah late the next morning as she rummaged through a rack of dresses in Julia's Boutique. "The gala is in three days and you have nothing to wear?"

"I have options at home," Leah reminded her, pulling a black sheath off the rack. "You just didn't like any of them."

"Not for the Gingerbread Gala. You're one of the hosts." Irene made a face at the black sheath. "That ruffle is—just, no. Put it back."

Leah hadn't been fond of the oversize ruffle, either, but no way was she going to wear the amethyst number Irene pulled off the rack. It was silky, sleeveless, and too fancy for her to ever wear again. "I'll freeze in that."

"It'll be warm in Hughes House, with all those people crowding inside." Irene waggled the hanger, making the dress swish. "Try it on, at least. The color's gorgeous on you."

Leah appreciated the compliment but couldn't see herself in the dress. "I don't think I'll be comfortable in something that shimmery."

"I guess it makes sense that you've got to be comfortable, but you're not wearing your Crocs to the Gingerbread Gala." Irene rolled her eyes.

"Ooh, this is pretty." The forest green dress was festive… But not her size. "Irene, this would look great on you."

Irene's eyes widened. "I'm going to try it on. Grab some things to try on, too, and meet me in the dressing room."

With Irene occupied, Leah rubbed the back of her neck and sighed. Finding something to wear to the gala had not been on her radar at all, considering how many other things had to be done. None of the guests would care what she wore, but they would be sure to notice if they ran out of food, or if there wasn't a gingerbread house in the foyer.

Oh, that gingerbread house. This morning she and Irene had finished the last shingles on the roof and the shredded wheat "shrubbery" before moving the house to its spot on the round table in the foyer. She'd known Benton would've helped, but the truth was, Leah wasn't sure she was ready to see him today.

Which was not at all sensible. They were partnered for the gala. More than that, they were friends, the sort that confided in each other. It was easier to talk to him than it was to Irene. But last night, for a moment—a long, lingering moment—she'd thought he might kiss her.

Or she might kiss him. Which would have been worse.

That's why she'd decided they'd better stop work last night and go home. She was so tired, she'd probably imagined any signals on Benton's part. He wasn't interested in relationships, after all. And she had a no-pastor rule.

He was a good man, yes, but that meant he deserved a good woman who wanted to partner in his ministry, not resent it. Grateful as Leah was for pastors and their families, she didn't want to live like that again.

"Not quite finding what you want?" Julia, the lithe blonde who ran the boutique, hung a cluster of patterned blouses on a T-stand.

"No, even though everything is pretty." Leah bit her lip. She'd already tried a few other places in town and come up empty. If Julia's didn't have anything for her, she'd have to drive out of town.

Julia examined the floral Leah had pulled out. "I assume this is for the Gingerbread Gala? I'm so excited about it, by the way."

"Yes, and I'm glad you're coming. I saw the flyer in your window. Thank you."

"It's going to be fun, and a town museum is a worthy cause, even if it means saying goodbye to my little exhibit up front." Since Widow's Peak Creek lacked a museum, each store on historic Main Street had given up a corner or cabinet to display artifacts appropriate to their building's original, 1850's occupant.

In Julia's case, her building had originally been a café, so a small glass case up front showcased a set of chipped dishware, a tin pitcher and a yellowed menu. "I've grown so fond of it that when we do get a museum someday, I'd like to keep the exhibit case and show something café related, or at least some teacups. I love how it ties us to our heritage as a gold mining town."

"I do, too. I'm sure Faith will have a good idea how

to help with that." Faith's Finds, the antiques shop, was directly across the street.

"I'll have to chat with her. In the meantime, you need something special for the Gingerbread Gala. You just haven't found The One yet," Julia enunciated. "I have something in the back that might work, a new arrival I haven't brought out yet. Willing to give it a look?"

"Why not?"

She'd always heard a person knows The One the moment they meet him. Or the dress, in this case. The moment Julia brought the scarlet dress out from the back, Leah had to agree. Sometimes, things really were that easy.

Even if matters of the heart were not.

After making their purchases, Leah and Irene stepped into the cool morning, bags in hand. "Not to brag or anything, but we're going to be knockouts at the gala." Irene winked. "Let's celebrate with lunch."

"You pick the place, but first I want to pop two doors down for a Christmas gift for Grandma." Christmas was in a week, after all, and Leah had been derelict in her shopping.

Within seconds they were inside Precious Time, the tiniest shop on Main Street. Clocks of all types, from digital to cuckoo, hung on the wood-paneled walls, and the cabinets were full of watches and trinkets. A tiny Christmas tree graced the shop counter, and the place smelled of cedar and pine. Irene's forehead bunched. "Does your grandma need a clock? I didn't think she was telling time anymore."

"No. I was thinking of something else." Leah stopped at a cupboard of music boxes.

"I used to have one of these. Not this nice, of course. Mine was hot pink and had a plastic ballerina inside."

"I had one of those, too." Leah had loved the rotating ballerina so much she'd pushed on it and broken the spring. "I thought Grandma might enjoy a music box that plays a hymn or song she recognizes. It might give her a few minutes of pleasure now and again."

Irene squeezed her in a sideways hug. "I love that idea."

Five polished, wooden boxes played hymns, but Leah's eye also caught on a few boxes that, when opened, revealed a tiny holiday scene. "Should I go with 'Amazing Grace' or one of the Christmas ones?" The one that played "Silent Night" was especially pretty.

"If you do the Christmas one, you can give her the other one for her birthday."

"I'll do that, then, and come back in June to get the hymn box."

"You may not be living here in June," Irene reminded her.

Oh. True. Leah's joy at picking out the box deflated. She would miss Widow's Peak Creek and the friends she'd made here. "I'll visit."

"I'll hold you to it." Irene frowned while Leah paid for the box, though.

Her transaction complete, Leah tucked the small bag into the larger one she'd received from Julia's. "Success. I'm ready for lunch."

"You might want to invite your man to come." Her tone hushed, Irene nudged her in the arm.

"What man?" Leah looked up in time to catch Benton and Jarod entering Precious Time. She gave Irene a quick glare that said he-is-not-my-man.

After greetings all around, Jarod rubbed his hands together. "You're looking at the newest sales associate at The World Outside. Tom just hired me."

"Congratulations." Leah included Benton in her smile, sure he felt relieved his brother had found work. Benton's return smile didn't reach his eyes, though. He wasn't happy about it?

"I start Monday." Jarod's chest puffed out. "Great guy, Tom. Gotta say, I'm looking forward to the employee discount."

"Oh, yeah? Are you a big camper, or are you into a sport?" Irene mimed holding a paddle. "I love to kayak."

"Never tried it, but I'm up for anything. Benton thinks I'm an adrenaline junkie. One of these days I'd like to free-climb Half Dome in Yosemite."

"No way." Irene waved her hands. "I know someone who's planning to do that once the snow melts."

"How's the gingerbread house? Anything I can do to help?" Benton stepped closer to Leah, allowing his brother and her friend to chat. This close, she could see how dark the circles were beneath his eyes. They hadn't been there last night.

"Irene and I took care of it this morning."

"Anything else I can take off your plate?"

She shook her head. "I'm off work all next week, so I'm available to coordinate last-minute things. I don't have Maude's phone number to ask about the gingerbread, though."

"I'll call her when I get home." Benton rubbed the back of his neck. "I read that newspaper article, by the way. The one that mentions us getting Hughes House."

"Me too. I wish the details about Rowena giving us the house weren't divulged in it, but otherwise it's a nice article. This morning, I checked our ticket sales and noticed a bump." Wow, he looked weary. "Are you all right? Please tell me you didn't pull an all-nighter in the parish hall."

"Not that, no." His laugh was mirthless.

Oh, dear. If not the parish hall, had he been called back to the hospital to be with a parishioner? Poor Benton. "Great news about Jarod getting a job, right?"

"Yeah. I'm happy for him." He sure didn't look like it, though. Shouldn't he be more excited? He must truly be tired, to show such a lack of enthusiasm.

"The cat came out of nowhere," Jarod was saying to Irene. "I'm an animal lover so of course I swerved, and boom, my car's totaled. Now I've got to bum off Benton for rides."

Leah's heart leaped to her throat. "You had a car accident? When?"

"Last night. Thankfully Benton was able to come pick me up."

After they'd finished the gingerbread house? No wonder Benton looked so weary. He'd had a difficult, worrisome night with his brother.

"I'm thankful you weren't hurt." Since Leah's parents had been killed in a car crash, she was always a little sensitive when the topic came up.

"It's all good, right, brother?" Jarod clapped Benton's shoulder.

Jarod's touch seemed to flip a switch inside Benton. He forced a grin—she'd never once seen him stretch his lips like that, not even when the mayor insulted them—and held up his hands. "We won't keep you two ladies."

"We're done now." Irene tapped Leah playfully on the shoulder. "And I'm ready for lunch."

Leah recognized the cue for her to invite the men to lunch, but once glance at Benton told her he was not interested in sharing a meal right now. Was he tired from such a late night, dealing with the aftermath of Jarod's accident? Or... Was he tired of being paired up with Leah?

"We'd better get going, Irene. Saturday lunch special at Emerald's." There. She'd dropped the name of the restaurant down the street so Benton and Jarod could come if she'd read the situation incorrectly. But she didn't think she had, not the way Benton offered a half wave and turned toward the store's counter before she and Irene had fully stepped away.

"You should've invited him." Irene sounded disappointed once they were out on the sidewalk, cool air nipping their cheeks.

"I see plenty of Benton these days, but how often do you and I go to lunch anymore?" Truthfully, all the gala work had kept her from investing in time with Irene. Leah swept her boutique bag so it brushed Irene's. "So what shoes are you going to wear with that green number?"

Talking shoes would keep the conversation off Benton, which Leah preferred. His walled-off vibe may not have anything to do with her. But then again, it could. And she didn't like how that felt.

"Why are we here again?" Jarod examined a cuckoo clock on the wall, a hand-carved wood piece decorated with birds, leaves and pine cones. "You're going to give one of these to Dad for Christmas?"

Nice as the clock was, Benton shook his head. "I thought I'd get him a meat and cheese basket from The

Olive Tree, actually." The store next door sold local olive oils and gourmet foods, and Benton liked the idea of giving his dad something nutritious to make a few lunches out of. "I'm looking for a gift for someone else."

"For that nurse friend of yours that was just here? Lee Ann?" Jarod's voice held a teasing edge.

"Leah, and no. It's not for her."

"Whatever." At least Jarod didn't pry further.

The proprietor, a middle-aged man with fading red hair, looked their way. "Can I help you with anything, Benton?"

"Not quite yet, George."

"I'll be back in a moment, then." George ducked into the back room.

Jarod sighed. "When we're done here, I'd like to borrow the car."

"I have to go into church and work on the parish hall." Odell Donalson wanted a progress update at church tomorrow. "What do you need it for?"

Jarod flicked the price tag hanging from the cuckoo clock. "Catching up with some old friends."

"Oh, yeah? Who?"

"No one you'd remember, little brother." Jarod shrugged. "But if this is you still being suspicious about me, never mind. I should've known you wouldn't take my word for it."

He'd clearly hurt his brother's feelings when he'd come to pick him up from the accident site and asked if he'd been drinking. But he'd been within reason. Jarod might not have had alcohol on his breath or displayed any obvious signs, but he'd been far too exuberant in his behavior. And far too cold, with blue fingertips and a bad case of the shivers. The thought occurred that Jarod could've been sitting in the damaged car for an hour or two after he crashed, giving the alcohol time to leave his system. No one would have been the wiser, since he'd driven off the road in a remote stretch of Raven Road.

So he'd asked if alcohol had been a factor, and offended his brother. *No alcohol under your roof. I heard you, man.*

Clearly, despite apologizing this morning and driving Jarod to interview at The World Outside, their relationship had taken a hit. Benton stared at his brother, who didn't make eye contact. "I'm sorry. I am. Can we discuss this later?"

"Nah, I'll just start walking home now. Exercise'll do me good. Don't work too hard on that glamorous job of yours, okay?"

As Jarod left, Benton gave a mirthless laugh. He'd blown the chance to build trust with Jarod, but at the same time, he couldn't ignore the feeling in his gut that there was more to the story.

Nevertheless, he shouldn't lose sight of the big picture. *Thank You, God, that Jarod wasn't hurt.*

As for working today in the parish hall, glamorous or not, Benton had no choice. It was still an unfinished mess. He'd gone home wound up over his inconvenient feelings for Leah, and then Jarod crashed his car—

The proprietor returned from the back room. "Any questions?"

"Thanks, yes." Benton pointed at what he wanted. George helped him make his purchase with a minimum of fuss or chitchat, which was fine, since his mood was so off. He had to get to the parish hall, anyway.

The rest of the weekend, except for Sunday services, he worked on the parish hall stage and floor. Odell wasn't pleased by Benton's progress, or lack of it, but Benton kept on a steady pace. *Lord, please grant me the energy and time to finish this up before Friday evening. I want to give the people of Good Shepherd the pageant they deserve.*

Much as he wanted his parishioners to be in a pretty, overhauled parish hall, though, his heart wasn't in his efforts. Since Friday night, everything felt different. With Jarod, absolutely. His brother avoided him, shutting himself in Benton's guest room. With Leah, too. Their only communications had been brief, about Maude and the gingerbread cookies, or confirming times and division of labor. He thought about confiding in her, but what was the use? He hated to burden her when she had so much on her mind, between the gala and her grandma.

It was best if he did as he always did and dealt with his burdens by himself.

Benton didn't feel much better about anything on Tuesday, the twenty-first of December. Gala day. It arrived cold and clear, with frost on the grass and roofs, appropriate for the first day of winter. Benton took the day off, leaving ministry needs in the care of a retired clergyman who helped from time to time.

When he arrived at Hughes House, Leah was already there, setting up a resin Nativity scene on the parlor coffee table. Dressed in jeans and a tree-green turtleneck sweater, she looked up at him and smiled. Her sweet face was like balm to the troubled spaces in his heart.

"Look what I found on the third floor, Benton."

He set the down the large pastry box he was carrying to examine the Nativity figures. "Beautiful."

I thought the house definitely needed it among its decorations."

"It did." Benton needed it, too. The reminder of what this holiday was about. Wonderful as the Gingerbread Gala was for the town, the museum and even for Rowena, it was window dressing for the true meaning of Christmas. So simple, and yet so powerful, and he'd allowed the busyness of the season—and his concerns and circumstances—to eclipse his gratitude.

"I'm glad you found it. It's the one thing our decor lacked." *Forgive me, Lord. No matter what's going on, I don't ever want to forget You.*

"Heads up, Ralph's out back." Leah stood up. "What's that in the box? It's not from Angel Food Bakery."

"Gingerbread people. I stopped by Maude's to collect them. The rest are in my car."

"Oh, I didn't think they were going to be ready until this afternoon. I can't wait to see them." Squealing, she lifted the lid, releasing the delectable fragrance of ginger and cinnamon. "They're adorable. I like how she packaged them, too, in these little cellophane bags."

"Yeah, she did great." His voice sounded unenthusiastic.

"You don't like them?"

"No, I do. I'm just—tired." Tired and unable to stop thinking of what a poor job he'd done with everything lately. Putting God first in his life. Caring for the physical plant of the church. Getting his family in order. "I'll start bringing in the boxes."

"I'll help you." She followed him into the foyer.

"It's okay. You finish up what you were doing."

"Did you see the gingerbread house? It's all finished."

He hadn't even thought to look at it. "Sorry. Wow, it's amazing." It truly was. A hundred times better than the one they'd made at the rec center, which still sat on his breakfast bar. It wasn't professional quality, maybe, but it looked neat, sweet and like a miniature Hughes House, exactly as they'd hoped. "You and Irene did a great job on the bushes and the roof."

"Are you sure you're all right?" Her words stopped him from going back out the door. "If I ever do something to upset you, or you want to talk about anything, I'm here. Like you said, we're friends."

He shoved his hands in the front pocket of his hoodie. He did trust her. He wanted to tell her. But it wasn't like he had proof Jarod had driven under the influence, so why share suspicion? Besides, his time with Leah was almost over. The gala was tonight. After this, Hughes House would go on the market. She'd be moving away with her grandmother.

He'd far rather spend their fleeting time together in another way. Like making her smile so many times, the image would be etched in his brain forever. Shaking aside his gloomy mood, he thanked God for every moment he'd have with Leah from here on out.

He smiled. "We are friends. Thank you for the offer, Leah, but it's okay. I'll get the boxes inside, and you finish up with the Nativity. Lunch is on me today. How about gingerbread?" He gently shook the box.

She smiled, as he'd hoped she would. "Talk about a sugar high that'll crash right when the gala starts."

He grinned and hurried out to his car.

He focused on laughing with her over the next few hours while they transferred the cellophane bags of gingerbread people into red wicker baskets and placed them beneath the tree in the foyer. They dusted furniture, vacuumed, received the chairs they'd rented to accommodate guests in the music room and fielded phone calls, including one from a reporter named Ellen from the newspaper, wanting to talk to them tonight. Afterward, he ran to Pickles' Deli to grab them lunch while she set up a table with activities for children, including board games, coloring pages with crayons and Christmas sticker sheets.

With Ralph for company, he cleaned the kitchen for the caterer while Leah swept the porches. They set up the rental chairs, tested lights, glued loose bows and set out a basket for tickets, which Irene had offered to collect. Benton signed for the snow machine while Leah received delivery of the mugs and stemmed glass flutes they'd rented for hot chocolate and sparkling apple cider, respectively.

At a certain point, there was nothing left to do but get ready themselves. Leah put Ralph on his leash and grabbed her purse. "I'm running home to change and grab a quick dinner before the caterer gets here."

"See you then." Before leaving the house, though, Benton checked his cell for messages and emails, finding none for the first time that he could remember. It was like all of Widow's Peak Creek was preparing for the Gingerbread Gala.

Then he called home. Jarod should have walked home from work by now—

"Hello?" His brother's voice answered.

"It's me. I'm going to grab some burgers. What do you want?"

"I'm heading out actually."

"Aren't you coming to the gala with me?" Benton

had bought his brother a ticket. They'd planned to go together.

"Gala? Yeah, I'll meet you there later."

"Don't you want a ride?"

"I'll catch one from a friend." Jarod's smile could be heard over the phone. "Don't worry about it, little brother. I know this night is important to you."

How could Benton not worry? Was Jarod avoiding him because he'd been drinking?

No, he knew better than to jump to conclusions. *Pray and don't think the worst. Trust God to handle this.*

"All right, then. Bye." Benton would trust his brother and grab himself a burger. But he'd better do it quick, before the guests arrived and found him in his hoodie and paint-spattered jeans.

Chapter Eleven

Leah arrived at Hughes House before Benton, welcoming the catering staff before heading upstairs. She flicked on the battery-powered candles in the windows, turned on lamps and ensured the rope blocking off the staircase to the third floor barred entry—only the first two floors would be accessible to guests tonight. On her way back down, the hair at the back of her nape lifted, drawing her gaze up.

Dressed in a tailored dark suit, crisp white shirt and a tie in holiday green, Benton stood in the foyer, gazing up at her with such intensity that she feared she must've smeared dust on her new dress. She looked down at once, brushing her skirt. "Am I a mess?"

"On the contrary. That dress is—" He didn't finish, smiling and shaking his head.

She came down the stairs, slowly, considering she wasn't accustomed to wearing heels. Or dresses this fancy. Even though it was short-sleeved, the thick fabric kept her warm. She'd accessorized with a short necklace that matched her sparkly shoes, but the most festive part of her ensemble was the cherry color of the dress.

It was probably the color that had stumped Benton and left him at a loss for words. "The dress is…red? Crimson? Vermilion? Santa-suit scarlet?"

"Beautiful." Then Benton's cheeks turned Santa-suit scarlet, too. "Perfect for the gala."

Surely, he was being nice, so she deflected with humor. "Thank you. The best thing about it is the pockets." She shoved her hands inside them to demonstrate, making the midlength skirt flare.

"What is it with women and pockets?" His lips parted in an amused smile. "Just kidding, I know, I know. I've taken pockets for granted every day of my life."

"Good answer." She laughed. "You look pretty sharp yourself." Boy, did he.

"It's a new tie."

"It's also crooked. May I?"

"Please." He lifted his chin.

Fingers trembling, Leah adjusted his necktie. It took all of two seconds, but in that short period of time she'd caught by the scent of cologne, musky and rich amid the gingerbread and pine scent of the house. She'd also noticed he'd shaved away his five-o'clock shadow and his hair was still damp from a wash.

It would be easy to fall in love with Benton. The easiest thing in the world.

But she had to fight it. Say something. Do something. Something normal. "The caterers are here," she said.

The front door swung open wide, and Irene stomped inside on tottering heels, Phil behind her. "Where's the party?" Irene laughed.

"You've come to the right place." Benton reached for her coat. "I'll hang this in the main bedroom's closet. Is that okay?"

"Sure thing." She handed it to him and he took the stairs two at a time.

"I'll go warm up." Phil kissed Irene's cheek before heading toward the music room.

"Well, well, well." Irene's grin stretched to her ears. "What did we walk into?"

"Nothing. I fixed his tie." Leah fixed her attention on the gingerbread Hughes House. One of the candy trees was ever-so-slightly askew.

"When will you get rid of your no-pastor rule?"

"Never. Not that he's interested in me, anyway."

"Oh, he's interested."

"I'm going to make sure the catering staff puts someone in charge of the hot chocolate station." She rushed to the kitchen, Irene's laugh filling her ears.

The next hour passed in a blur of activity. While she replaced the battery in one of the candles in the parlor, Benton rushed past. "I forgot to set up the wheelchair ramp. Don't forget to grab a stuffed mushroom before they're gone. They're for you, you know."

"Don't you forget a hot wing."

He stopped in the threshold. "Very funny. For the hoedown, I remember."

"I'm serious. I called the caterer and added a small tray for you. They're in the kitchen."

"Seriously?" He whooped and ran outside.

"I like hot wings," Irene said wistfully as the front door shut behind Benton. "And he totally likes you and you like him. I think you should give it a chance. Maybe it won't be like you think it will." Irene didn't press the point, but instead gathered the ticket collection basket and the guest list.

Maybe it won't be like she thought it would be. Maybe it could be better, even.

A hundred questions tumbled in Leah's brain, but this wasn't the time to think of them. Every other concern fled as Rowena sauntered in through the front door, a vision in silver sequins that sparkled brighter than her bedazzled cane. Marigold had driven her, as well as a few friends Leah recognized from CRV who trailed in after them. Benton brought up the group. His hesitant smile matched Leah's emotions right now.

Would Rowena like the candy house?

Rowena's gaze didn't scan the marble table, though. Instead, she reached for Leah's and Benton's hands. "The house is exquisite. I had a peek the day you decorated, of course, but to see it now, at night, with the lights on the banister and the tree? Magnificent."

"It's like being in a Dickens story," Marigold exclaimed.

"That's what Leah said on the first day we visited." Benton met Leah's gaze. "This house was made for an old-fashioned Christmas, complete with a horse-drawn carriage in the drive. But the house is wonderful for a twenty-first-century Christmas, too."

"Old and new go together perfectly at Christmas." Rowena grinned at the tree. "I must get a closer look." She dragged them toward the tree, but her steps faltered at the marble table. "My word. The gingerbread house."

As Rowena peered at it, her expression inscrutable, Leah exchanged nervous glances with Benton. Did she hate it? She must, the way she just stared without smiling. Disappointment pooled in Leah's stomach. "I'm sorry we couldn't get a professional one made."

Benton's smile was sympathetic. "I really blew it

on this section of the roof. Why don't I hide it in the kitchen? Leah, do we have something else to put on the table."

"We do. Poinsettias and candles will look a lot more elegant."

"Hide this? Why would we ever hide the most adorable thing I've ever seen in my life?" Rowena clutched their hands harder, lifting them in the air like they were watching a football game and their team scored a touchdown. "Girls, did you see this? The kids made a little Hughes House."

Marigold grabbed Leah's free hand. "I'll be jingle-belled," she said in her elf voice.

"Look at the shutters." Rowena tutted. "Green cookies."

"Benton found those," Leah said. "Wasn't that smart of him?"

"Leah baked the dough."

"It's glued together so well," Rowena marveled.

Benton winked at Leah.

Voices carried from the front porch. The first notes of "The Holly and the Ivy" trilled out from the music room. Servers carrying trays of savory appetizers emerged from the dining room, and Irene opened the door to welcome guests.

The Gingerbread Gala had begun.

Benton had a hard time moving from the foyer, since so many people greeted him, it felt like he was stationed at the church door after a church service.

"This is our second date without the baby." Kellan shook Benton's hand. "She's home with Paige's mom."

Paige bit her lip. "I can't stay for the whole gala,

160   *A Small-Town Christmas Challenge*

though. Poppy's only seven weeks old and I can't be apart from her for long."

"Seven weeks already? Enjoy every minute." Tom Santos glanced at his six-year-old twins, Logan and Nora. "That phrase 'grow like weeds' didn't come out of nowhere. One day they're babies, and the next?"

"We're in first grade!" Nora announced, swishing her tartan skirt.

Faith, Tom's fiancée, smiled indulgently at the kids. "Turning seven soon, too."

Benton clapped Logan's shoulder. "You're taller every week, dude." Then he gestured that they should move farther into the house. "Don't forget to take a bag of cookies before you go. They're in the baskets beneath the Christmas tree."

From that moment on, Benton was on the go, comforting one of the servers who spilled half a tray of bacon-wrapped shrimp, ducking into the kitchen for a few hot wings and ensuring the solar backyard lights had come on, all while chatting with guests.

Leah was equally busy. He spied her sweeping up shards from a broken mug, showing off the gingerbread house to Clementine and her nephew and niece, Wynn and Annie, and pointing out the gingerbread cookies to Maude.

Twice they crossed paths on the staircase, taking folks up for tours of the second story, although Faith was doing a much better job explaining the history of Hughes House, the Victorian-era furnishings, the town, and even Christmases past. She'd been stuck in the upstairs bedroom that Rowena's husband had converted to a library almost since her arrival, fielding questions.

He'd just finished telling Tom where his fiancée,

Faith, was when he found himself on the opposite side of the foyer from Leah, their first moment this evening without a single demand on either of them. She looked so beautiful in the glow of the Christmas lights, her red dress the perfect complement to her coloring and dark hair, which she wore in a soft style.

It wasn't the lights or the dress that made her so striking, however. It was the glow in her eyes, the fullness of her smile, her gentle, sweet nature. It was the way she made him feel, like his heart was going to pound a hole through his rib cage.

She stepped toward him. "Had any hot chocolate yet?"

"No time for that, Leah," Irene rushed out from the dining room. "The hot chocolate guy is having some sort of personal emergency, and in the parlor, there's a woman with a food allergy asking about the appetizers."

"I'll take the hot chocolate guy," Benton said.

"I'll tackle the allergy question. Which reminds me, did you get a hot wing yet?"

"And bacon-wrapped shrimp. Did you get a mushroom?"

"Four." Leah grinned.

"What's that all about?" Kellan followed him into the dining room.

"Inside joke."

"I figured that much. I was referring to the way you two were looking at each other, especially since our talk the other night."

All right, yes. Benton was drawn to Leah, but this was not the time or place. "Catch up later, okay? I need to talk to the hot chocolate guy."

The poor kid's left cheek pooched out like a chipmunk's. "My wisdom teeth came out on Friday, but it's really hurting me, man. Sorry."

"Aw, man. Could be dry sockets. Go home and call your oral surgeon tomorrow. I'm sure someone else on the catering staff can cover you, but I'll stay here until then."

"No, you won't," Kellan said, stepping behind the hot chocolate station. "You've got enough other things to do. I've got this until we have to get back for Poppy's bedtime meal." He consulted his watch. "Forty minutes."

"Thanks, my friend." He spoke to the caterer, found a replacement for Kellan and was promptly grabbed by Maude.

"Odell's not happy with you." Her stern expression was a stark contrast to the word *joy* stitched in bold letters on her holiday sweater.

"I hope he's enjoying the evening, nonetheless. And you are, too."

"Me? I suppose."

"Have you sung any carols yet?"

"Pfft, no. I can't sing."

"Everyone can sing at Christmas. Come on." He escorted her to the music room, where they sang with the group gathered around the piano. After "Hark, the Herald Angels Sing," he checked his watch. He should touch base with Leah. Where was she? He headed to the parlor.

Leah wasn't there, but Rowena beckoned him. She stood with a round-cheeked woman in her sixties. "Benton, meet Olive Vance. She grew up in the staff house at back."

He'd forgotten all about her coming tonight, but

her being here was a treat. "I hope you're enjoying the party."

Olive's bright blue eyes crinkled when she smiled. "This was such a fun place to grow up. We had our own home, of course. I hardly ever came through the house."

"There was a separate entrance," Rowena explained to Benton, "but it was fenced over in the eighties. Seemed silly to have it when no one lived in that house anymore. A lot has changed since those days, but tonight, Hughes House is in her glory again, just like I hoped it would be. You and Leah did a wonderful job, Benton."

Benton started to demur, but Olive waved him off. "This place is packed, and every person here is thrilled for the experience. And all the proceeds will go to such a good cause. Well done."

Those two words were the ones Benton always ached to hear from his dad, but never had. His greatest hope the past decade and a half had been for his Heavenly Father to say those words to him. To be pleased with him. Olive's words sparked that longing in him for God to approve of Benton's life, his work, his ministry. And how he took care of his family.

Maybe this Christmas would be the time he could help his dad and brother learn more about God. Maybe this year, the cycle would break, and they could move forward on the solid foundation of Jesus.

But tonight, he had other obligations, pleasant ones, too. He gestured toward the back of the house. "Would you like to see your old home, Olive?"

Her gray curls wobbled from her enthusiastic nod. "Rowena, are you coming?"

"Oh, yes. I heard the kids put lights on the porch."

With Olive on one arm and Rowena on the other, he strode to the back door—not through the kitchen, but the door behind the foyer, watching for Leah all the while. Ah, there she was, tapping her watch and looking for someone. Him.

She looked up. He wagged his eyebrows, and she gave him a thumbs-up. As Benton escorted the ladies outside, he could hear Leah's voice talking to the children. "Let's look at the lights out back."

The temperature was somewhere in the high forties, but neither of the ladies on Benton's arm complained of cold. Instead, they marveled at the Christmas displays and solar lights, their laughter curling into clouds of vapor.

"Look at my house." Olive giggled like a little girl. "It's beautiful."

"You know what would make it better?" Benton glanced back, finding Leah among the groups of guests she'd drawn outside. At her signal, he smiled at Rowena. "Snow."

She laughed. "It would, wouldn't it. Alas."

Behind Benton, a mechanical whir started, followed by a chorus of *aahs*. "Turn around."

Small white bubbles floated down from the machine, positioned atop a tall stand, with the soft, slow grace of snowflakes, a few at first, then thicker.

"Snow!" Olive shouted, holding out her hands to catch the snow bubbles. Logan Santos ran around the yard whooping with his best friend, Wynn Nelson. Logan's twin, Nora, spun in a circle, holding hands with Wynn's little sister, Annie, singing a song about snow from a Disney movie. The adults weren't immune to the fun, either, laughing and clapping. Even Phil and Irene opened their arms and hands to the snow. It wouldn't last or produce a snowman, but no one seemed to mind. It looked like Faith even wiped a tear from her eye.

Grinning, Leah hurried toward them. "Are you surprised, Rowena?"

"Yes," Rowena said. "You two have thoroughly, deeply blessed me. Thank you."

Benton returned Rowena's hug, and then Olive's, and he couldn't help it. He hugged Leah, too. "We did it," he whispered in her ear.

"We did, didn't we?"

He didn't want to let her go.

"Benton? Leah?" A woman in a dark coat strode over the grass, a camera hanging on a strap over her shoulder. "I'm Ellen Brouhagh from the newspaper. We spoke on the phone this afternoon."

Benton reluctantly released Leah. "Yes, thanks for coming."

This is amazing. I got some good shots of kids playing, but I'd love one of you two, and Rowena, of course. Maybe inside the house, for variety?"

"By the Christmas tree, of course," Rowena said. "And we can discuss the museum fund."

With everyone out back for the snow, the house was hushed, peaceful. A calm settled deep into Benton's heart. Was it the joy on the kids' faces? The feeling of a job well-done? Or, as he stood beside Leah in front of the Christmas tree they'd decorated, something akin to hope?

It wasn't hard to smile for Ellen's photos.

His smile slipped as the front door burst open, however. Mayor Judy Hughes barged into the foyer, looking like the angel on top of the tree in that gold dress.

"You might want to call the police, Pastor Hunt," she said before he could offer any words of welcome. "Your car's being broken into by a pair of drunkards. That is your gray sedan right out front, isn't it?"

Most likely it was indeed his vehicle, but no matter whose car it was, he couldn't allow someone to steal it. Pulling his cell phone from his pocket, he rushed out the door and leaped down the porch steps.

Sure enough, two figures fumbled with the driver's side door, shuffling and talking with raised voices, not seeming the least bit concerned about being caught. He ran toward them. "Hey!"

Two faces looked up, illuminated by the house lights. Two familiar faces.

"Jarod. Dad. What are you doing here?"

"Ben, there's my boy." Dad lacked a coat, and his gray hair was mussed.

"Dad?" The mayor's attempt to look apologetic failed. "I didn't realize it was your own family. But isn't it interesting? Nineteen years ago you stole your brother's car. Now he and your dad are stealing yours. History seems to be repeating itself."

Chapter Twelve

Leah's limbs went cold, but it had nothing to do with the chill of the evening. Mr. Hunt, a stockier, older version of Jarod, had come to town, without warning. And something was not right with him.

Mr. Hunt waved a newspaper. "This is your new house? Pretty fancy, son."

Benton had told her his dad often asked for money. Is that what this was about? He'd seen the article about her and Benton receiving the house? Her heart filled her throat.

Benton took his dad's shoulder. "It's not that simple, but we can talk about it later. Jarod, did you know Dad was in town? Is that why you're so late to the gala?"

"I'm late because I don't have a car, remember? I walked here from my friend's house and found Dad wandering around, which is as big a surprise to me as it is to you. I couldn't let him come in like this, could I? I was going to drive him back to your place in your car, but he's fighting me on who gets to do the driving. He took the keys from me."

That explained what the mayor had seen, then. Leah

knew Jarod had keys to Benton's car. But what did he mean *like this*?

Mr. Hunt swayed on his feet, and then she understood. He'd been drinking.

As a nurse, Leah had seen the terrible grip substances could hold over people and the heavy toll it could take on their families, and she felt compassion and heartache.

But hearing that he wanted to drive? Knowing he could kill someone? Her parents' car crash hadn't been caused by a drunk driver, but that didn't matter. She wasn't cold anymore as anger radiated from her core to her fingers and toes.

"How dare you?" Her heels smacked the drive as she marched to them. "Drunk driving kills innocent people, Mr. Hunt."

"I'm not drunk," he protested, his words slurring together. "I don't touch the stuff anymore."

Before she could call out his obvious lie, Mr. Hunt slipped to the ground, slumping against the driver's side door of Benton's car. Leah's nursing instinct took over. Kneeling, she pressed two fingers into Mr. Hunt's cold, damp neck. His pulse was rapid. "Mr. Hunt? Can you hear me?"

"Dad?" Benton was at her side, voice tight, gripping his dad's hands. "His name's Richard."

"Richard, look at me." Unbuttoning his collar to make it easier for him to breathe, her fingers brushed warm metal. She withdrew a silver pendant stamped in red letters and her pulse accelerated to match his. "Oh, no."

"What?" Benton looked up at her.

"His medical alert pendant says he's diabetic." She

ran her hands over Richard's pockets in search of glucose tablets but didn't find anything but his wallet. "Someone get a glass of apple cider. Quick."

"I'll do it," the mayor said. Leah glanced up at Benton. "Call 911. I think your dad is in insulin shock."

"I didn't even know he was diabetic." Benton's tone was shocked, but his fingers were steady when he dialed for emergency services. Jarod mumbled he didn't know, either.

Within seconds, Mayor Hughes returned with a flute of cider. Leah lifted the glass to Richard's lips. "Take a sip, please. Good. One more."

Thank You, God, that Richard is conscious. It would take several minutes for his blood sugar to rise, but already his eyes seemed better able to focus on her. As she offered more juice, she met his gaze. "I think you're hypoglycemic, Richard. You should be fine, but to be on the safe side, we're calling an ambulance."

He blinked, as if telling her he understood.

"I'm staying on the line until the ambulance arrives." Benton moved the microphone away from his mouth but kept the phone to his ear.

"I don't understand what's going on." Jarod brushed his dad's graying hair from his brow. "What's the deal with juice?"

"He may have skipped a meal or… I don't know, there are several possible causes, but his sugar's low. He was telling the truth. This isn't alcohol related." Shame filled her chest, hot and thick. "I'm sorry I jumped to that conclusion. Benton, I should've given your family the benefit of the doubt, same as you do."

Jarod shook his head. "You shouldn't have given it

to me, Ben," he whispered. "My accident. I lied. There was no cat. I'd been drinking."

Benton's eyes shut. "I wanted to believe you, but I think I knew. All weekend, you could've told me. It's been hard to hear you lying to me."

So much made sense now. She'd known something was bothering Benton. "Why didn't you tell me?"

"I didn't want to burden you."

"Burden me?" Her voice came out strangled. "I thought—"

Richard shifted. She refocused her attention on the patient, making him comfortable, asking him questions to gauge his responses. Benton's decision to not confide in her was none of her business, anyway. Except that they'd discussed Jarod's accident, and she thought they were the sort of friends who divulged things to one another. After all, he'd told her why he'd driven Jarod's car nineteen years ago. Not even Kellan knew that. She thought she was… Special.

Clearly she wasn't. And it hurt.

She wouldn't make it worse now by answering the question in Benton's eyes. The one where, if she were truthful, she'd have to admit she cared for him as more than a friend.

The ambulance arrived, its red-and-blue lights illuminating the house and the small but curious group gathered on the drive, watching them.

People were curious and concerned. She understood that. But the way the people grouped under the Christmas lights reminded her too much of the night in early December when she was in middle school, when neighbors were drawn by the police cars in front of her house. They stood and watched, but did nothing to help or comfort Leah's family in their greatest moment of terror and grief.

How awful, someone had said back then. *Poor kids.* And the worst question, *How could God let that happen to a pastor of all people?*

People gaped and grappled while she fell apart, and she was still angry about it. Those old feelings of resentment rose in her chest all over again.

This wasn't the same, though. Mayor Hughes fetched juice, hadn't she? If Irene had known what was going on, she would have leaped to lend aid. No, this was an entirely different situation.

Leah wasn't a child anymore, either. She shouldn't respond to tonight's events through the same lens. But it didn't help her emotional state that those painful memories tangled with her current feelings. Angry at Jarod for having driven while under the influence. Most of all, though, she was angry at herself, for falling for Benton when she'd known there was no future for them.

She had a lot to unravel in her heart and mind, with God's help. Much as it would hurt to leave Widow's Peak Creek, it was for the best. She needed a fresh start.

But first she had to get through the evening. She wouldn't desert Rowena. Or Benton, either. She couldn't completely step away, even if they hadn't shared anything beyond the Gingerbread Gala.

Pacing in the ER waiting room, Benton felt sick, both to his stomach and at heart.

How long had Dad had diabetes? Why hadn't he shared this news with his sons? Benton would've helped… The way he helped urge his family to avoid alcohol? Dad had probably been afraid Benton would nag him to watch his diet and test his blood sugar.

And then there was Jarod. His older brother sat in a chair, staring at the floor. Benton had a lot to discuss with him, but this wasn't a good time, not with Dad back in triage. Still, the fact that Jarod drank and drove Friday night made Benton's jaw clench so hard it hurt his molars. Jarod had endangered himself and others.

He'd also hurt Leah in his effort to avoid burdening her.

On top of all that, he'd failed to give Rowena the perfect Gingerbread Gala. He'd had to take his leave long before he'd intended so he and Jarod could get to the hospital. Leah had stayed behind to close things down, and thankfully, the fake snow had been planned to cap off the evening, anyway.

While most of the guests had still been enjoying the soap snow and hadn't seen the ambulance, word had spread. His cell buzzed with texts. Kellan asked if he could come, but Benton declined.

It's going to be fine, but thanks. Stay home with your wife and baby.

Marigold and Rowena both texted. Benton's fingers typed the same words to both.

I'll keep you posted. No need to come, we're fine, but thank you.

It was better that he was alone. With Jarod, of course, but they were together and apart at the same time. Each lost in his own thoughts. The way they were accustomed to being. Self-sufficient, as they'd been since they were kids growing up with an alcoholic dad, who was absent emotionally and physically. That was how they'd learned to be adults, by doing for themselves.

Benton had come to learn that God was an ever-present source of help and love, and he prayed as he paced the ER floor. But just because he'd accepted God's help didn't mean he needed other people's.

An inexplicable pull drew his gaze to the sliding entrance doors. Leah and Irene stood inside them, their gala finery peeking out beneath the hems of their bulky coats. Leah's gaze darted around the waiting room, searching. For him.

Much as he knew it was best to handle everything alone, he was filled with relief at seeing her.

"Any news?" Leah's face was etched with concern.

"Not yet." Happy as he was for her presence, shame rolled over him. He'd dumped so much of his family's troubles on her.

"If it's any comfort," Irene said, "your dad should be fine. It's a good thing Leah was there, though, or he could've had a seizure or gone into a coma."

"Thank God you were there, Leah." He offered praise for God's provision. "Did the gala end okay? I'm sorry I left you to close it down."

"Don't be silly." Leah shook her head. "Honestly, it ended right after you left, and on a high note, too. The snow machine rental guy was fast, and the caterers were ready to go. The cleaning crew will be in tomorrow. There was nothing there for you to do, anyway."

"I'm going to check in on Jarod," Irene said. "Excuse me, guys."

"How are you holding up?" Leah's voice was low as

she watched Irene cross the waiting room. "Can I get you some coffee?"

"Thanks, no. I'm keyed up as it is."

"Would you like to pray?"

She was asking to pray with him? For him? So many came to him requesting prayer, but so few prayed for him. It felt strange to accept the gift, but he nodded.

Leah didn't touch him, but as he shut his eyes, he could feel her gentle presence beside him. It wasn't a long prayer, but it was heartfelt. His agitation lessened. "Thank you."

"I'm sorry I accused your dad of drinking, Benton. I came at him hard."

"It's okay. I get it."

Her hazel gaze searched his face. "None of this is okay. What can I do to help?"

"You already did so much, helping Dad."

"What can I do right now, though?"

"Nothing, really." He'd burdened her enough already.

"More company," Leah said, her gaze fixed on the entrance. Benton turned. Odell and Maude charged toward them, their brows grooved with worry lines.

"Thank you for coming," he said. "We're still waiting for news, but Dad should be okay."

"That's good, but that's not the only reason we're here." Maude folded her arms. "There's trouble."

Something wrong at church? With a parishioner? His phone hadn't buzzed with news of an emergency, but Maude looked mighty upset. "What's happened?"

Maude grabbed his elbow. "There's gossip that you have trouble with alcohol and stole a car when you were a kid? Who would spread lies like that?"

"Not now, Mother," Odell said, much to Benton's relief. But then he turned on Benton. "I'm sorry your dad is sick, but I hope this won't interfere with your ability to finish work on the parish hall."

"Are you serious right now?" Leah folded her arms. "Benton's dad is back there receiving treatment, but you're here because of the parish hall?"

"It's all right, Leah." Benton appreciated her defense, but he was so accustomed to being peacemaker, he couldn't stop now. "Odell knows I'm committed to my job."

"What about your family?" Leah gaped at him. "Surely your parishioners understand your priorities include your father."

So that's what this was about. Her past. "I can see to both, Leah."

Maude snorted. "I don't know why I ever worried you two would pair up. She'd never make a good pastor's wife, talking to parishioners like that."

"Maude," he warned.

"No, she's right." Leah sighed. "Rest assured, Maude, Benton was my partner in this Gingerbread Gala thing, but that's all."

Not even his friend, eh? That was a kick in the gut.

"You're not harping on this matchmaker stuff now, are you, Mother?" Odell rolled his eyes. "The pastor has enough to take care of with his family's troubles before he can take on a wife. Especially not someone as vulnerable as Clementine, with those two kids."

As if Benton would knowingly hurt Clementine, Wynn or Annie. It had been something else Odell had said, though, that sent a flash of incandescent rage through Benton. Odell had no way of knowing, but he had echoed Katie's words from long ago. Words Benton lived by. *You can't have a family of your own until you get your existing family in a good place.*

"Look, Odell, that's uncalled-for," Leah's voice was almost a growl. Ever quick to come to someone's defense.

"It's okay, Leah. Odell is right." He'd started to forget, but it had taken tonight to remind him. "My priorities are my ministry and my family. I've messed up." He'd failed his family and his parish. "I'll get everything handled, Odell."

"The family of Richard Hunt?" A female voice called from the triage door. He spun to see a woman in scrubs propping the door open with her foot, gaze scanning the waiting room. "Come back, please?"

Benton lifted his hand in acknowledgment but felt obligated to say something to Maude, Odell and Leah. "I appreciate you coming by. Good night." He hurried to meet Jarod at the triage door.

Before he walked inside, though, he glanced back at Leah. She looked sad, like she wanted to say something, but then she turned to leave with Irene.

Watching her leave the ER, he ached, because she was leaving his life, too. But this was for the best. For both of them.

Lord, give me strength.

Chapter Thirteen

Within twenty minutes of leaving the hospital parking lot, Leah and Irene curled up in their stocking feet on Leah's couch, fluffy blankets over their laps and hot mugs of chamomile tea in hand. Ralph snuggled between them, his warmth comforting. Leah stroked his forehead while she filled Irene in on everything, from the events of the Gingerbread Gala nineteen years ago to tonight.

Was she breaking Benton's confidence? She hoped not, but weary and heartsore as she was, she needed a friend. "You won't say anything about Benton's past, or his family's addiction issues, will you? Especially if you hear others gossiping about it?"

Irene mimicked locking her lips together and throwing the key over her shoulder. "I hate that someone's spreading rumors about it. I mean, talking about an ambulance coming is one thing, but it doesn't sound like the stuff going around is even accurate."

"Pastors live in fishbowls."

"People gossip about others, no matter what their vocation." Irene sipped her tea. "Odell and Maude were wrong about everything tonight. You would make a good pastor's wife."

Leah's denial sounded like a duck's quack. "I'm not the least bit diplomatic."

"I don't think there's a single personality type that makes an effective ministry spouse. I would think love of the Lord would be the most important thing, and love of your husband. And you and Benton—"

"Irene." Leah didn't want to hear it.

"Okay, fine. But another thing, you're a helper, hon. You jump right in to be of assistance. You care about what's right. And you stomp out gossip." Irene tapped her foot on the plush rug like she was squashing a sparking ember. "Speaking of gossip, I'll change the topic and just say it's interesting that the story about Benton crashing into Rowena's car wasn't common knowledge. There must've been plenty of people at the Gingerbread Gala that night."

"I guess, like tonight, the guests were otherwise occupied when all the fireworks happened."

"And by fireworks, you mean Richard trying to get into Benton's car, right? Because I didn't think you could top the fake snow, but fireworks would've been something." Irene chuckled.

"No real fireworks, but I guess I did sort of explode," Leah admitted. "I misjudged Richard."

"I would've too. The behaviors can overlap."

"I didn't misjudge Jarod, though. I wish Benton hadn't believed him."

Irene sipped her tea. "It's not bad to look for the good in people, Leah. Even if they've failed you before."

Leah tried to push Irene's words out of her mind all night as she tossed and turned in bed, but it proved impossible to escape into sleep. She certainly didn't agree with Benton's decision not to have a family of his own until his family was solidly in recovery. Jarod was drinking again, so that could be a long way off. Besides, Jarod's sobriety wasn't Benton's choice. It was Jarod's.

But Benton loved his brother. She could hear it in his voice that night they'd sat on the grand staircase at Hughes House, after polishing off a pizza and antipasto. She smiled, thinking about the fun they'd had that evening, admiring the Christmas tree. They'd had a lot of fun working together on the gala.

Mulling over the past, however happy the moments might have been, would not do any good, though. Now that the gala was over, she and Benton could sell Hughes House. She would take her portion of the sale and move on.

She'd forget Benton eventually. She had to.

Benton yanked off his green tie and shrugged out of his suit jacket, ready to make a bed for himself on the living room couch. In the few hours since leaving the hospital, they'd swung by Church Street, looking for Dad's car, so Jarod could drive it here to Benton's house. Dad had planned to check into one of the bed-and-breakfasts in town, but Benton didn't like the idea of him being alone. Not after the health scare he'd just suffered, so he set up Dad in his bedroom.

Now Benton spread sheets and blankets over the couch. Tired as he was, though, he didn't feel like sleeping. The cushions were comfortable—he'd had many a good Saturday nap here—but tonight, he sat up, wide-awake, starting at the dark hulking shadow of his Christmas tree in the corner. "Leah's not coming over to decorate you now," he said out loud. Then he scrubbed his hands over his face.

You're tired. You've got a lot to do tomorrow. You've got plenty of things to worry about besides Leah, who you never could have been with, anyway.

But everywhere he looked in his house, he saw Leah—and she hadn't even been inside before. Their first gingerbread house still sat on his breakfast bar. Every breath he took was tinged with spruce, reminding him of their tree-shopping day and their plans to decorate it. He tried hard to ignore how beautiful she'd looked tonight in her red dress.

Stop thinking about Leah and pray about how to fix these messes.

He didn't sleep much, but when the first purple-gray fingers of dawn poked through the window shutters, he tossed aside the blankets. He might as well get an early start on the parish hall. Sitting up, he caught a glimpse of a dark object on the coffee table. The nativity set. A familiar sight, but this morning he paused to look at it.

Jesus was helpless that first Christmas, an infant, dependent on others. By choice, so He could identify with His people, but also teach them about His purpose and His love.

Benton's mind flashed back to the Scripture sampler at Hughes House. *The Lord is my strength.* He'd thought he'd made God his strength, thought he relied on Him, but had he ever fully let himself be reliant on the Lord?

Not on purpose, no, probably because he struggled with the concept of relying on a father. He knew God was faithful, but his earthly father wasn't, and despite having good intentions, Benton had still tried to force his own will into being. Not that the things he wanted were bad. His family's sobriety and salvation were good things.

But he wasn't responsible for their choices. It was prideful to think that he could change anything. Katie, his old girlfriend, might think him a hypocrite as a pastor because his family wasn't picture-perfect yet, but—

Yet? They'd never be perfect, because they were regular people in need of a Savior.

Benton bowed his head and prayed, repented, asked God to help him rely on Him alone. When he was finished, he didn't have all the answers, but he did have peace and the determination to make things right. And he'd need help to do that, especially with his family. Later today, he'd investigate resources for family members of alcoholics. First, though, he coveted the prayer of others. It would require vulnerability, but maybe admitting his own brokenness wasn't a bad thing for others to see.

To that end, he picked up his phone.

"Hey, Benton, just talking about you." Kellan was hard to hear over the hum of voices in the background. Wherever he was, he was surrounded by people. Was he out to breakfast? He couldn't possibly be at the bookstore he ran since it wouldn't open for a few hours. Even if Kellan had opened shop early because Christmas was three days away, there wouldn't be such a big crowd at this hour.

"Are you all right? Where are you?"

"Funny you should ask." Muffled laughter spilled over the line. "We're at Good Shepherd."

"What's wrong?" Panic filled his chest. "I'll be there in five minutes."

"Nothing's wrong." Kellan's tone was light. "And

you don't need to be here at all. The doughnuts are almost gone, anyway—hey, you missed a spot about a foot up, Phil. Tom, there's an empty spot to your left."

"Phil? Tom?"

"Irene's boyfriend and Tom Santos."

They weren't even his parishioners. "What are you guys doing at church?" How'd they even get in? No one had keys but Benton and the office staff, who weren't due in to work for another hour. "Is Jan there?"

"No, she's still sick, but she gave me the key and alarm code last night when I dropped by her place. As to why we're here, it's too long a story when I'm holding a wet paint roller."

"You're working in the parish hall?" Benton sank against the couch. "But I'm supposed to—you didn't need to do this."

"Let us bless you, brother. You shouldn't have to bear everything by yourself."

It was an answer to prayer, only he'd never expected God to provide for him before he'd even uttered the words.

Chapter Fourteen

Benton shook his head as he took in the scene. The parish hall was an absolute mess. But soon? It would be a fully refurbished space.

Tom stood atop a ladder with a paint roller, while Faith used a brush to go over spots near the ground. Tom's kids, Logan and Nora, played a board game on the stage with Wynn and Annie Nelson, while their aunt Clementine painted around the kitchen door and Kellan and Phil painted the far wall. Marigold stood at the kitchen door, waving a dust rag at him. "Welcome to the painting party."

This was wonderful, amazing, beautiful. And painful, too, because all this support and help had been here all along, if only he'd asked for it.

Kellan's brow knit in concern as he met Benton. "What, did we do it all wrong?"

Benton clapped Kellan's shoulder. "It's exactly right. I don't understand how you pulled this off, or how you knew about any of this." Hardly anyone knew.

"After the snow last night, Leah said your dad showed up but was sick and you took him to the hospital. Then Tom overheard Maude and Odell talking about all the parish hall repairs you're supposed to be doing. I had no clue what that was about, so I asked Odell. He said the stage and floor were finished, but you were painting the whole parish hall yourself. We all talked about it last night. You had a lot on your plate with your dad being in the hospital, so you shouldn't have to do this, too. In fact, it didn't seem right that you were doing this all by yourself, anyway."

"I agreed to it, though."

"Before the gala happened when you had more time on your hands, and that agreement didn't include the paint, according to Phil, who heard it from Irene. But even then, you didn't need to go it alone."

"It was my job, but you're right. I kept it to myself out of pride." And to that end, he needed to talk to Kellan. "A little later, there's some stuff I want to tell you. About me."

"Yeah, I heard you stole a car, right?" Kellan rolled his eyes. "Some people will repeat anything."

"Well," Benton began.

The outer door opened, and for a half second, Benton expected Leah to walk in, her bright smile soothing the jagged places of his heart. They hadn't parted well last night. He needed to make things right with her before she left Widow's Peak Creek.

However, it wasn't Leah, but Jarod and Dad. Neither of them had ever visited Benton's church, not this one or his first assignment, and their presence made him smile. "Hey."

"We got your note, son, and thought we'd grab you before we go to Del's for breakfast."

"Glad to see you out of the hospital." Kellan wiped

his hand on his paint-specked jeans and offered it to Dad for a shake. "I'm Kellan. Your son is an amazing guy."

"Really?" Dad didn't seem to know how to take that news.

Jarod looked around. "Didn't know you'd be in the middle of a painting party."

"I didn't know, either. They did this to surprise me."

"That's nice. Nicer than anything I've ever done for someone."

"That's not true." Benton led him away from the others, who'd stopped painting to talk to Dad. "You did a lot for me when we were kids. Took the heat off me more than once when Dad was in a mood."

"I got you in trouble plenty, though, too. Like the night of the Gingerbread Gala when I left you to take the blame."

"I chose to drive."

"To protect me. I ran away like a coward. I'm still a coward. Lying to you about everything." Jarod rubbed his forehead, as if it ached to recall past events. "Truth is, I lost my job because I was drinking again. You probably figured that out already, though. I'd never trust me again, if I were you."

"Are you willing to talk for a minute? Frankly?" At Jarod's nod, Benton guided him outside onto the church patio, away from the noise and glancing eyes. They sat on the cold concrete planter around an oak tree. "Last night, the mayor said it was history repeating itself. A Hunt stealing a car from his brother. She's wrong, of course, but there were similar elements, right?"

"Like me still being a disaster."

"No, I mean Dad might not be drinking now, but he's still not taking care of himself, still wants money—

he saw the newspaper article about me getting half of Hughes House and that's why he came last night. You're still struggling with your addiction. And I'm still trying to force you guys to do things you don't want to do. Each of us has problems, Jarod. Troubles, trials. You've got a tough row to hoe as you work on your sobriety, for sure, but we aren't the same kids who had to fend for ourselves. We have resources, and we have each other. And God is right here. I'm going to rely on Him to help me, help you, okay?"

"What are you talking about?"

Benton stretched his legs out. "I can support you and give you tools. And you'd better believe I'm praying for you. But you have to *want* to change."

"I want to. I want to move on from this. Be sober, hold down a job." Jarod stretched out his legs, too. "Speaking of work, my shift starts at The World Outdoors pretty soon. I was going to treat Dad to breakfast, but if you're still working in the parish hall later, I'm happy to lend a hand. And maybe tonight we can talk. Really talk."

An answer to years of prayer. Benton's heart was so full, it felt as if his chest might explode.

They returned to the parish hall, and Benton was surprised more people had arrived. Odell and Maude.

It didn't take more than a second to realize they hadn't come to pitch in, though. Odell glared down at the linoleum. "These are patches, not replacements."

"Because the entire floor should be replaced." Benton held his hands up in a peaceful gesture. "My portion of Hughes House's sale is going to church repairs, and I didn't want to waste money on linoleum that will hopefully get replaced soon, anyway."

Kellan shook his head. "You're seriously giving your half of the money to the church? Why am I not surprised?"

Odell fisted his hands on his ample waist. "I hope you don't think that by funding repairs you can make decisions without committee approval."

"Of course not, Odell. I'd never—"

"I don't know what you'd do, to be frank. You didn't keep your word about executing these repairs yourself. You fell behind and pressured parishioners to cover your failings."

"That's not what happened here," Marigold protested. "Benton had nothing to do with all of us showing up."

"But I'm grateful all the same." Benton made eye contact with everyone who'd come to help. "Odell, we can talk in private about this further, if you'd like, but the bottom line here is the parish hall will be completed in time for the pageant. We can all be thankful for that."

"I don't want to talk in private. Everyone should hear what I have to say." Odell's jowls quivered. "Mayor Hughes confirmed that you did indeed steal a car and alcohol abuse played a factor. You should have told us."

Benton ignored the gasps in the room. "The elder board knew about my crash when they hired me. But while I broke the law driving without a license, technically, I did not steal the car. It belonged to my family."

"He was covering for me," Jarod announced, his voice shaking. "Because I'm the one with the alcohol problem. I was going to drive on that night you're talking about, so Benton took the wheel. I ran away when he crashed into Rowena Hughes's Cadillac. He protected me."

Benton wrapped an arm of support around Jarod's

shoulders. Glad as he was that his brother admitted the truth, however, Benton had to deal with Odell right now. "I hid the truth about Jarod's role that night from many people, so you're right, Odell. I've failed. Too many times to count."

Odell sneered. "Then maybe we should have a different pastor."

The words hung in the air like storm clouds, dark and heavy. Maude's face crumpled into tears. Clementine glanced nervously at the kids, but they were the only ones in the room unaware of what was going on, giggling over their game.

"Come on, Odell," Kellan began. "That's ridiculous."

Marigold stomped her foot. "Odell Donalson, that's fool talk."

"No, it's worth considering." Benton felt no panic, only peace. "If the church prefers another pastor, I understand. I'm still paying for the flooring and other delayed maintenance, though, and I'm going to help this fine bunch of folks with the parish hall, after I say goodbye to my brother and dad. Excuse me."

Jarod and Dad followed him out to the courtyard. "Wow," Jarod said, once they were out in the cool air.

"If you've come into money, son, no need to do this job anymore." Dad hitched his thumb back at the parish hall.

"About that, Dad." Benton faced his dad squarely. "Like I said inside, when Hughes House sells, I am not keeping the money. It's all going to church repairs and what's left goes to the missions fund. I'm not keeping a cent."

"Not even a pinch for your old man?" Dad laughed like he was joking, but his eyes told a different story.

"Just to get me on the right track. I'm going to go back to work, son. Jarod said he'd help me. I'm going to stick to my plans this time. I'm gonna change."

"That's wonderful, Dad." He'd heard the story several times before, but he prayed this time would be different. "I have a lot to do here, but let's plan on dinner tonight. I'll cook." Benton took his dad's shoulder. "And Dad? I'm here for you. You can stay with me as long as you like, both of you. But as I told Jarod, my love, prayers and encouragement are the only sorts of help I can give. Change must come from you. You and God, if you let Him."

Dad nodded but didn't look Benton in the eye. "See you at dinner, then."

Benton watched them leave before he returned to the parish hall. Would Odell and Maude still be inside? How would the others react to him now that they knew he and his family weren't, well, perfect?

Thinking about it that way, Benton could only laugh at himself. God had known all along.

The truth might cost him friends and his job, but he wasn't worried. God would work everything out somehow. He felt lighter, freer. The only weight on his shoulders was the way he'd parted with Leah.

He had to make things right, one way or another. But how?

Leah curled up on the chair by Grandma's bed, singing with her to "Silent Night" as it played on the music box. It might still be three days to Christmas, but Leah was glad she'd given Grandma this one present early. She was certainly enjoying it.

Despite the disastrous way last night ended, Leah

was having a good day. She had the week off work, so she'd enjoyed a leisurely morning with Ralph before coming to see Grandma. Later, she'd drop by Hughes House to ensure the cleanup crew had locked up, but she wouldn't go inside. She wasn't ready yet. Soon, she'd have to undecorate the tree and the house. She'd expected to share the load with Benton—

She wouldn't think of it now. Not when Grandma was singing. She knew all the words, and her gray eyes sparkled.

Leah's cell phone buzzed. Rowena's name came up on the screen, along with a thank-you message for the Gingerbread Gala. Leah was about to respond when a second text came through.

Did you hear about Good Shepherd?

What about it? Had something happened at the church? Was Benton okay? Leah's pulse ratcheted as she typed out her response asking what had happened.

The parish hall got done this morning thanks to friends helping Benton complete it.

Surprise spread through Leah's chest, calming her erratic pulse. *Thank You, Lord.* What a burden that had been to Benton. She might not be in the best place with Benton right now, but she would never wish him ill. On the contrary, she wanted the best for him.

That didn't mean she wanted to talk about him right now, however. She'd better cut this off before Rowena asked about him.

I'm with Grandma now. Check in later?

Rowena's response was swift.

Of course, but I ask one thing more. My ride to Marigold's Christmas Eve supper fell through. Would you drive me?

Leah smiled at the numerous Christmas emojis Rowena used.

No problem. It's not Santa's sleigh, but my car knows the way.

Grandma inched out of bed. "What a pretty sky out the window."

Leah tucked her phone back in her pocket and closed the lid on the music box. "It sure is bright blue today. Would you like to sit by the window?"

"That chair, there." Grandma pointed to her favorite seat.

Leah settled Grandma in the chair and sat beside her, taking in the view of the cloudless, clear sky, the creek and the walking path beside it. A young mother with a trio of children took advantage of the mild weather, bustling along the far side of the bank.

"Look at those kids." Grandma tapped the window. "I'll have to take my Bruce to the creek when he gets home from school. He's such a rambunctious boy."

Leah's heart sank to her stomach. Bruce, Leah's dad, hadn't been a little boy in a long, long time. Worse, he'd been gone nineteen years now.

Her parents had been out of her life six years longer than they'd been in it.

She gasped at the realization. Pain roiled up from somewhere deep within her—

No. Leah pushed it down, further, further, the way she always did when it threatened to consume her. For years now, she'd welcomed the busyness of her job and other activities, because they'd kept her too occupied and weary to think about what she'd lost. To grieve. She'd had to be strong, first for her younger brothers, and then, as Grandma began to show signs of failing, for her.

Boy, was she feeling everything now, though. All the grief and loneliness and despair she'd forbidden herself now pushed up to the surface. The pain was unstoppable, despite her best intentions to hold it back. Hot tears leaked from her eyes.

She banished them with a brusque swipe of her hand. *No more tears!* But the flow thickened, stinging her eyes and slipping down her cheeks.

Waves of grief crashed over Leah. This was hard. So, so hard. She'd been carrying on alone for so long. She missed her parents. She missed her brothers. She missed Grandma, missed all she'd lost to this wretched disease. And she missed Benton, even though she shouldn't— and she was not going to think about him right now. It was all too complicated, and thinking about it made her cry harder.

She turned away, not wanting Grandma to see her tear-streaked face.

"What is it, dear?" Grandma's warm hand settled atop hers.

This was the first time in so long that Grandma had

asked her anything. Touched her. Even if Grandma didn't know her, her gaze was tender, concerned. Should she answer?

Leah swiped her tears with the back of her free hand. "I'm sad today."

"You poor duck. Try not to worry. God is real, you know."

Leah knew it, of course, but hearing Grandma say it, something shifted inside of her. She hadn't fully embraced the reality of His presence, had she? She'd wanted to put off her pain, but in doing so, she'd closed herself off not only from healing but His role in it. He hadn't abandoned her, though. He was faithful, and instead of her trying to stand strong on her own two feet, He offered His strength to her.

And joy, even in times of despair. She'd missed so much by not trusting Him with her past.

Was she doing the same thing when it came to her future?

Leah would have to pray about it, but right now, her grief was overwhelming, pouring out of her along with her tears. *You were here for me all along, but I ignored Your hand of comfort. I'm sorry, Lord. Please forgive me.*

Leah would cling to Him with all her might, now and in the future. Together, they would face this pain inside her. And though it ached to the depths of her being, she felt hope, too. Like maybe now she could start to heal.

After her sobs subsided, she reached for the tissue box and dried her face. Then she squeezed Grandma's warm hand. "Thank you for everything you've done for me. You gave me a home. Encouraged and supported me, and my brothers, too. You loved us. I love you and I will always be grateful for you."

"What a sweetheart you are. Being thankful is good." Grandma returned her gaze out the window. "I like the creek."

"You do, huh?" Smiling, Leah blotted away another round of tears.

"Cissy and I waded in it all the time, even in winter. Our toes were blue." She chuckled at the reminiscence of her sister. "Mother was so angry when she called us out of the creek. Cissy obeyed, but I didn't. I told my mother I'm never leaving this creek. And I meant it. See? I'm still here."

Out of the creek, of course, but not away from it. Grandma had grown up, married and raised her family in this town.

Grandma tugged her hand free of Leah's. She didn't say anything, but the wary look in her eyes made clear that she wasn't comfortable holding hands with a stranger. She'd already forgotten that she'd initiated contact with Leah a few minutes ago.

Leah forced a smile. Grandma studied her a moment, then returned her gaze to the creek. She was quiet, but she soon wore a faint smile.

Leah stayed with her a while longer, savoring the time together and mulling over a thought that had implanted in her head while Grandma was talking.

This close to Christmas, Leah hoped the Creekside Retirement Village's executive director was still in the office. She needed to talk to him, now.

Chapter Fifteen

The following day, Leah spent more time in prayer than she had in recent memory. She took a long walk with Ralph along Widow's Peak Creek, had lunch with Irene and talked on the phone with Rowena. That night, her sleep was sweet, and she awoke on Christmas Eve refreshed and ready to enjoy the day the Lord had made.

She chatted with her brothers in the morning, and in the afternoon, attended the service at her church. She wasn't scheduled to drive Rowena to her dinner at Marigold's until late afternoon, but Rowena invited her to come early to chat, so Leah did, popping by to spend an hour with Grandma first.

Her time with Rowena was delightful, and the conversation didn't drift to Benton once, other than Rowena mentioning the parish hall's completion and Benton's dad feeling much better. It wasn't that Leah didn't want to talk to Benton. In fact, she had a lot to say to him. She wasn't sure if he wanted to talk to her, though. Leah resolved to let the Lord handle the Benton situation in His time, but for now, she was glad Rowena didn't pry.

The light began to change outside the apartment window, prompting Leah to check the anniversary clock. "It's almost time to leave, if I'm going to get you to Marigold's."

"We have a few minutes. Finish your tea."

Obediently, Leah sipped the remainder of the holiday blend, an herbal fusion of peppermint and other spices. "A perfect end to a good day."

"But the fun is just beginning, Leah. I'm only starting to feel like it's Christmas."

"Only now?" Rowena's apartment was thick with Christmas atmosphere. Multicolored blinking lights flashed from the small artificial tree on the end table, and a candle on the coffee table gave off the spicy aromas of cinnamon, orange peel and cloves. "Because of your dinner and the pageant afterward?"

"There's nothing like a Christmas pageant, but everything's just…special." Her hand flapped. "I'm glad I spent part of my Christmas Eve with you, Leah."

"I feel the same way." With a wink, Leah stood and carried their mugs to the kitchen.

Rowena lifted her coat from the back of the chair. "Thanks again for driving me."

"My pleasure." Leah shrugged into her coat, unplugged the Christmas tree lights, blew out the candle and grabbed her purse in the time it took Rowena to adjust the collar of her coat in the mirror.

"Ready?"

"Ready." Rowena grabbed her cane, then stopped. "I forgot to blow out the candle."

"I did it." The stinky smoke still lingered in the air. "Christmas lights are off, too. You're good to go."

Rowena locked up the apartment with meticulous care, checking the double bolt three times. At last they were on their way, chatting as they walked to the lobby. Rowena's step seemed slower than normal, though. Was she tired? Feeling off? Under the lobby's bright lights, her color looked good, but Leah felt concerned. "Are you all right? Did you check your blood sugar?"

"It was fine. Now, Leah, you'll forgive me for not inviting you to Marigold's little party, won't you? I knew you'd have other plans."

Leah's heart panged as she opened the lobby door for her, letting her out to the parking lot. She did not have plans. Irene had a family commitment later, Leah's brothers had gone skiing and Grandma was asleep. How to phrase that she was alone without making Rowena offer an invitation out of pity? "Actually, no, but that's totally fine because—"

A loud snort interrupted her sentence. A strange, animal-sounding snort. Leah looked up.

A pair of horses hitched to a carriage parked—if horses parked, Leah wasn't sure—in the yellow curbed loading zone. Benton, wearing his heavy coat and the scarf he'd loaned to her at the Christmas tree lot, walked toward her, his smile hesitant. Hopeful.

Rowena rapped her cane on the ground. "It's fine because you *do* have plans tonight. If you're amenable to them. Forgive our trickery, won't you? My efforts at stalling were rather transparent."

Leah couldn't think straight with Benton's dark gaze boring into hers. "What is all this?"

"Remember what you said about a horse-drawn carriage at Hughes House?" He gestured behind him. "I wondered if you'd be willing to join me there for dinner. Not a long one, because I need to be at church early for the pageant, but I thought it might be good to see

Hughes House in its glory one last time. And talk. I don't like how we parted at the hospital, and there's so much I want to say to you, Leah."

She had so much to say to him, too, but her mouth wouldn't work. He'd rented a horse and carriage? For her?

Irene's car pulled up behind the carriage and she lowered the passenger side window. "Ready, Row?"

Row? How cozy had Irene and Rowena become without Leah knowing?

"I am, Irene, dear. If you're all right with this, Leah." Rowena's gaze was gentle. "We wanted this to be a surprise."

"You surprised me, all right." She smiled at Rowena and Irene, then at Benton. "Dinner would be wonderful."

His hand was warm as he assisted her into the carriage, his fingertips lingering when he let go to reach across the padded seat for a thick, buffalo plaid blanket. "This will keep your lap warm."

The temperature was the last thing on her mind. "Thank you. For the blanket and for this." Her sweeping gesture included the driver, who urged the horses out of the parking lot to the cadence of jingle bells. "Today's one of the busiest days in a pastor's year. You didn't need to do this."

"I wanted to. Sometimes when we're busy, we don't take the time to enjoy what's around us. To appreciate the moments before they pass."

"I've been learning that."

"I don't want to miss a thing tonight, though."

"Me, neither." Not the passing scenery, nor the presence of the man beside her. Even if some things weren't meant to be, she wanted a memory of him to cherish.

Every light and candle glowed from Hughes House,

welcoming them as they pulled into the circular drive. Benton hopped down and helped her descend. She greeted the horses with pats on the neck while he exchanged a few words with the driver. Then, so gently she might have imagined it, he touched her arm. "Dinner's ready."

They shed their coats and moved to the dining room, where the table had been set with a white damask runner, two china place settings and a stunning centerpiece of white poinsettias, pine and bayberry. A thin teal ribbon wove through the arrangement, the exact shade as the tiles around the fireplace.

"It's beautiful."

"I had help." He held out her chair for her. "Irene told me to decorate with white and teal. Not blue, not green. Teal. I told her you'd schooled me on how important shades are, so I chose the ribbon wisely."

"You did the flowers?" Wow.

"First things first." He gestured to a small silver gift bag beside her plate.

He shouldn't have. "This wasn't necessary."

"It's not for you." He didn't sit down, but stood beside her, his smile cheeky. "It's for your grandma. I hope she'll like it. Want to open it to be sure?"

Leah dug into the white tissue paper and pulled out a cardboard box bearing Precious Time's familiar logo. "Is this what you were doing when we ran into each other there?"

"It's a music box. It plays 'Amazing Grace,' and it's such a familiar hymn I hoped she'd like it. What's the matter?"

Leah's hand had gone to her mouth, and she realized Benton must have gotten the wrong impression. "You won't believe this, but I bought her a music box too."

"I can take this one back."

"No, you don't understand. I had to decide between 'Amazing Grace' and 'Silent Night,' two favorites. You couldn't have known, but God did, and now she has both. I'm so touched." She tucked the tissue back around the box and looked up at him. "Thank you, Benton."

"It's my pleasure, truly." He stepped back. "Hang on while I grab the potpies."

"Potpies?" Just like the first meal they shared. Was it a fitting bookend for this, their last meal together?

He returned, carrying a tray of two steaming potpies. "I hope they're hot enough. George and Sandy let me buy them frozen."

"I didn't know they sold frozen pies."

"They don't, but they made an exception for me. Shall we eat while they're hot?"

At her nod, he said grace. She poked into her crust, allowing savory steam to escape. "I've never had a potpie served on china before."

"I'm sorry it's nothing fancy. No big Christmas Eve dinner."

"I wouldn't want to eat anything else." It sure beat the leftover pasta she'd planned to microwave tonight. She speared a forkful of chicken and carrot. Once she'd swallowed, she smiled. "Delicious. And hot."

"Phew." Smiling, he dug in.

She had so many questions. So many things to tell him. *Where to start, Lord?* Perhaps with something easy. Something downright impersonal, even. "Have you heard from Faith? I glimpsed her at church earlier but didn't get to ask about the extra donations the museum council received at the Gingerbread Gala."

"Not yet, but I'm glad you brought it up. The gala,

I mean." His eyes softened. "I'm sorry for the hurt I caused by not confiding in you."

She took a deep breath to steady her nerves. "I overreacted. First accusing your dad, then getting angry at you. After all, you had no evidence to prove he lied to you, and there was no reason for you to tell me."

"Sure there was. We agreed to be honest with each other, didn't we? But I held back."

"When we agreed to be honest, we were talking about the gala, not our personal lives."

"It's hard to separate any of this from our personal lives, don't you think?"

She fiddled with her necklace. "You're right."

"I didn't just hurt you, Leah. I did it in front of other people, and I can't imagine how that must have made you feel. You've been so clear about wanting to avoid being in the public eye, so to speak. Being in a fishbowl again."

She had. It had been important to her since she was a kid. So important she'd created a rule for herself about not dating pastors. "I admit I noticed it, yes. I've preferred to have a boundary around myself."

"I didn't realize it, but I've built a boundary, too, to a degree. Wanting to look like the all-together pastor, where my family is concerned, anyway. I think some of that comes from being the kid of an alcoholic. I created habits to cope, not all of them healthy, to protect them and myself." He sat back in his chair. "I don't know if Rowena told you, but it's all out now. My accident all those years ago, Jarod's role in it, everything. The whole town probably knows."

Her heart ached at the thought of anyone giving him a hard time. "I'm sorry."

"I'm not." What a strange thing to say. Stranger still, he smiled. "Now the world knows I'm not perfect."

"You're not?" Her teasing tone made him laugh.

"Far from it." He grinned. "Not that anyone put me on a pedestal, but it's good for folks to be reminded everyone, no matter their calling, is a sinner in need of a Savior. Also, there's no fear of anyone finding out anymore. People are praying for me. It feels…really good."

"What if others judge you harshly, though? What if they betray you?"

"It would hurt a lot. Vulnerability requires risk, but it's worth it. Even though it means I might not be the pastor of Good Shepherd much longer."

Leah's fork fell from her fingers. "What?"

"Odell wants my dismissal, but so far no one's taken action to that end," he started. He couldn't get out another word due to the sudden pounding at the front door. "I have no idea who'd be here. It might be an emergency."

"Oh, dear." Leah followed Benton through the parlor and to the front door.

The group assembled on the porch had the general look of Christmas carolers, folks of all ages bundled up in coats and scarves. Leah recognized Kellan, Paige and baby Poppy, Clementine and her nephew and niece, Wynn and Annie, a few others, and was that Maude in the back? But unlike carolers, they weren't singing, and their faces didn't glow with holiday cheer. In fact, they looked downright downtrodden.

"Is it true?" An older woman's chin trembled. "You're really going to leave us?"

Chapter Sixteen

Benton froze, hand on the doorknob. Life in ministry was full of these moments, but this was the first time he'd felt so torn between two halves of his heart. This was precisely the sort of thing Leah didn't want in her life. These folks, his parishioners, were witnesses to the fact that he and Leah were having a private dinner. She was probably upset.

But until the people of Good Shepherd told him otherwise, he was their pastor. He smiled an apology to Leah, but she was busy beckoning the small crowd inside.

He took the hand of Kellan's grandma, Eileen, who looked near tears. "I'm not going to leave unless the church wants me to, and so far, I haven't heard a word."

"But Maude said Odell told you to leave. We want you to stay. You're our pastor." Clementine bit her lip. "We were afraid you wouldn't be at the pageant."

"That means the world to me. Truly." Benton's heart was about to explode. "But I'm definitely going to the pageant."

"Sorry, man," Kellan whispered, pulling him aside.

"Everyone at Marigold's was talking about Odell's suggestion that you move along. Maude was convinced you were leaving, and folks got upset enough to want to talk to you. Rowena felt she had no choice but to tell them where you were, thinking they'd wait until after the pageant, but they were afraid you wouldn't make it. I figured if you weren't coming, you'd have told me, but Paige and I decided to come along, in case we could help. I'm sorry we interrupted your time with Leah."

"No, Kellan, I'm sorry. You're my best friend, and yes, I would have told you, but the truth is, I should've told you the whole story about my car accident. Will you forgive me?"

Kellan responded by enveloping Benton in a strong embrace. "We're brothers. I'm here for you the way you're here for me."

"What a rotten few days you must've had." Paige shook her head in sympathy. In her arms, baby Poppy fussed, as if in agreement.

They were interrupted by Herb, an older widower. "I was going to give this to you tonight, but in case you weren't coming to the pageant, this is for your dad. I heard he's diabetic. Got this cookbook from Kellan's store. Receipt's inside if you want to return it."

"No, Herb, that's incredibly thoughtful. Thank you." He hugged him.

Clementine was next in line with a sheaf of notepaper in her hand. "This can wait, now that I know you're not leaving, but my best friend from high school is an alcoholic. It's been a tough time for her, but these are great resources that have helped me support her. I wrote them down for you."

"That's an answer to prayer, Clementine. Thanks."

"You were there for me when my sister died and I got custody of the kids. We're here for you, too." Clementine stepped back, extending a hand to Leah. "How's your grandma doing?"

Maude gripped his sleeve. "Marigold gave me a talking-to about how I listened to gossip, and even though some of it was true, I shouldn't have thrown it in your face. I'm sorry."

Benton's head spun. "That means a lot. Thanks."

"But you should probably direct a sermon at Marigold on bossiness. Odell would benefit from it as well since he's acting like such a turkey. Now, I suppose we can all get to the pageant instead of lollygagging around here."

"The pageant doesn't start for an hour yet, Maude," Kellan said.

"I'll be at church shortly," Benton promised. But another family stepped through the front door, Faith, Tom and his twins. What were they doing here?

"We were driving by and I was so excited to see you here, I insisted that Tom stop the car. I have to show you guys real quick." Faith dug into her purse and then handed a folded paper to Benton. "That's the grand total of what we took in for the museum because of the Gingerbread Gala plus a few donations."

Hefty ones.

Leah sidled in to view the page, as well. "This is amazing, Faith."

"We're so much closer to buying a place for the museum," Faith said.

"All right, kids, we'd better go so Pastor Benton can finish up here before the pageant." Clementine beckoned her niece and nephew, who'd gone to sit on the staircase with Tom's kids.

"The pageant's in an hour?" Tom glanced at Faith. "We already went to Christmas Eve services, but why not go to Wynn and Annie's pageant too? The kids would enjoy it."

"Can we?" Nora's eyes were big.

"Actually," Clementine said, "there's room for more sheep in the pageant, if you'd like to participate, Logan and Nora."

The kids responded in a chorus of happy shouts, hopping together out of the house and down the porch steps. He felt just as joyful, his heart full of gratitude at his parishioners' display of care. Except...

Leah.

When he shut the door behind the last of the impromptu guests, she wasn't in the foyer anymore. He followed the clinks of dishes to the kitchen, where she stood at the deep sink, rinsing the plates.

"I know we're in a hurry, but I thought I'd at least rinse things off before we left." Leah dried her hands on the thin hand towel hanging on the oven door. "What great news, isn't it?"

"The museum fund?"

"Yes, but I meant your parishioners."

"It is, but I have mixed feelings right now. That?" He waved his hand in the direction of the foyer. "That was exactly what you saw when you were growing up. Privacy intruded upon. Life in a fishbowl." *Lord, give me strength.* "I know you're leaving, Leah, but tonight I was going to tell you I don't want to be apart from you. I'd find a church close to wherever you're going to be. But God's called me to be a pastor. It's my world. And now I really see that even if you feel about me the way I feel about you, you'll never be with me."

An electric shock traversed Leah's spine and spread to her fingertips. "Dating, you and me?"

"I guess I didn't make that clear enough with the carriage ride."

"I didn't think—well, I thought you were doing something nice so we could tie up loose ends. But Rowena didn't tell you, I guess."

"Tell me what?"

"I'm not leaving Widow's Peak Creek. Not when Hughes House sells, hopefully not ever."

His eyes went wide. "What about your grandma?"

"She's staying, too." Leah blinked back hot tears. Since she'd started crying two days ago, the waterworks were quick to come. "She may not know me, but the day after the gala, it was clear she knew where she was. Widow's Peak Creek is her home. I can't take her away. So, I spoke to the executive director, who talked to the board. Instead of moving Grandma, I'm going to use my share of the Hughes House money to start an endowment for Creekside Retirement Village's new, expanded memory care unit. With more staff, tools and programs, starting with music therapy and an enclosed yard big enough to walk around in. Rowena approves, and we're putting together a board to oversee the endowment."

His face glowed. "I can't tell you how happy that makes me. For the town, for your grandma and other patients."

"We have to sell Hughes House first. To that end, I just had an idea." She bit her lip. "What would you think of offering it to a nonprofit at a discounted price? Like the WPC museum? What better space for a town museum than the oldest, grandest house in Widow's Peak Creek, just around the corner from historic Main Street?"

"For exactly the amount on Faith's financial sheet?" Benton grinned.

"It might not be market value, but it's enough for me if it's enough for you."

"It's more than enough." Benton's grin made her knees go weak. "Leah, that's almost the best news I've heard today."

"Almost? Your job being secure is the best?"

"No. The best news is you staying in town. Even if all we can ever be is friends. I hope you'll want to stay friends, that is."

"No more than friends because you're a pastor, you mean?"

"Yes. I won't ever push."

Of course he wouldn't. He was a respectful, kind man. The most wonderful man she'd ever met in her thirty-two years of life, and she didn't want to spend another day without him. Her lips stretching in a slow smile, she beckoned him out of the kitchen. "We have a lot to discuss, Benton, but first we have a pageant to get to, don't we?"

"We?" Following her, he shut off the kitchen light. "You don't have to go. There's time for me to take you home."

"You don't understand." She scooped Grandma's present off the dining room table. "I want to ride to church with you, and you can drive me home afterward."

He gaped. "If parishioners see us arrive together, though, they'll make assumptions."

"I know." Leah felt almost flirtatious, passing him out to the foyer to get her coat and purse. "That's all right with me."

He hurried to help her into her coat. "You're right, I don't understand." The light touch of his fingers sent a shiver down her neck.

"How should I put this?" She opened the front door while he donned his coat and shut off the lights. "All those people coming to see you tonight?"

"Yes?" He glanced at her while he locked the door.

"While I was with my grandma, having that realization that this was her home, I'd also come to see that I hadn't trusted God with my grief. I missed a lot by not relying on His strength. I've done the same with my future, pushing God out and making rules about who I can date, as if He isn't bigger than any set of circumstances or potential problems."

"Leah." His stare was deep as the sea.

"I don't see your parishioners as spectators on your life. I see people who love you. Who care what happens to you, who rely on you. I'd forgotten how privileged pastors and their families are to be part of people's lives." She stepped onto the drive, looking up at the stars twinkling in the ink-dark sky. "They even care about me and my grandma."

"What are you saying?" His voice held a hopeful, expectant quality she'd never heard from him before. Like he was half-afraid to believe what he was hearing.

"That I was wrong. I've been afraid of being hurt, but there's no guarantees in life, are there? I'm praying for God's help with being vulnerable. It's a risk, true, but some risks are worth taking." She took a deep breath. "Even falling head over heels for a pastor."

Was it wrong that she enjoyed rendering him speechless?

He recovered fast enough, though, his lips twitching. "Do you have a particular pastor in mind?"

"Maybe, but I'm open to suggestions." She couldn't help but tease.

He grinned, but the smile slipped. "I've missed so much, too, thinking I had to do everything myself. Fixing my family. Looking like a pastor's supposed to. Then God brought you into my life, and you both showed me how different life can be. But not everything's changing, Leah. Jarod's going to rehab right after Christmas, but you know addiction is a lifelong struggle. For my dad, too, and he's staying with me for a while."

"I have my own challenges, you know. Fears." They stood facing each other on the drive, so close she could see the bob of his Adam's apple when he swallowed. "But I'd rather face them with you and God than without."

"Shall we face the future and our fears together then? You, me and God?"

"You have fears? What are you afraid of?"

"Losing you." He lifted her hand to his chest, and beneath her palm, his heart pounded at a wild gallop. "Can't you tell? I love you, Leah. More than I ever thought possible to love another person. I've been alone for so long, but I don't want to be alone anymore. I'm not sure I know how to be a husband or father, based on my childhood, but I want to be the best of both of those, with God's help. And your love. Leah, I want to build a life with you."

She couldn't think straight, with his words sinking into her marrow and her palm on his beating heart. But she didn't need clarity of thought to tell him how she felt. "I love you, too. So much. So much I can't imagine another day without you."

Then his hands weren't holding hers anymore. One slid around her back to hold her close, and the other cupped the nape of her neck, his thumb tracing her jaw. He kissed her until she couldn't breathe, and when he pulled away, her fingers were tangled in his scarf, gripping for dear life.

"You do love me." His voice was low, marveling.

She answered him by tugging his scarf, pulling him close for another kiss.

When they broke apart, he kissed her cheek, her nose, her forehead, but Leah could tell his lips were stretched into a smile as he did so.

"Are you free tomorrow?" He was as breathless as she was.

"My Christmas Day is all yours. What did you have in mind?"

"I'd like to meet your grandma. And then, if you're up to it, I have an undecorated Christmas tree at my house in desperate need of your help."

Decorate a tree on Christmas Day? She'd never heard of such a thing, but Christmas wasn't about a day on the calendar, anyway. It was about so much more. "Sounds wonderful."

"Merry Christmas, love."

Oh, she could get used to him calling her that. "Merry Christmas."

Holding hands, they left Hughes House. It had never really been theirs, but in Leah's heart, it would always belong to them, to their story.

Looking at Benton in the dark, starlit night as they walked to his car, she knew she was home to stay.

There would be so much to tell Grandma tomorrow.

Epilogue

April

"Hughes House now belongs to us all," Rowena proclaimed, as she and Faith together used large silver scissors to slice a fat red ribbon tied across the porch. "Welcome to the Widow's Peak Creek Museum."

Leah met Benton's happy gaze as they applauded. After the pageant Christmas Eve, they'd told Faith about Leah's idea for Hughes House to be the museum site. The offer had been received with tears of joy and unanimous approval by the council. Rowena had loved the notion, too, and it hadn't taken long at all to set everything in motion.

The last time Leah had been inside Hughes House was the day of Faith and Tom's wedding reception back in January. It had seemed only fitting for the couple to hold it here, since the museum had started as Faith's personal project. It had also been decided that the museum would be available to rent for social events, and the Gingerbread Gala was already on the books for December 21. Now, at last, the museum was ready to open to the public. Holding hands, Leah and Benton made their way inside.

The house didn't quite look the same as it used to, with the downstairs furniture replaced by displays showcasing artifacts from the area's Native American history through the gold rush to the mid-twentieth century. Upstairs, a few rooms served as examples of what the chambers would have looked like upon Widow's Peak Creek's founding.

The other furniture had found new homes, either through auction to fund the museum or as donations to the local women's shelter. Rowena had insisted Leah and Benton each select one item to keep, however. The tea cart, complete with its collection of china teacups, held pride of place in Leah's living room, and the Scripture sampler hung on Benton's wall, reminders of Rowena's generosity, his mother and God's faithful care.

After they'd examined the displays and chatted with other attendees, Benton squeezed Leah's hand. "Would you like to go out back? The roses are blooming."

"Sure." It was a beautiful day, with bright sun, blue sky and a high in the low seventies. They passed numerous guests on their way out, but sadly, not Mayor Hughes. She was not as supportive as the rest of the town council, most of whom were here today. Benton led her outside and down the porch steps. Several children, including Tom's twins and Clementine's niece and nephew, ran around the lawn, playing some sort of game with plastic balls. Faith had been smart to provide activities for the kids. Leah waved at them as they strode down the path. "We'll have to tell Grandma all about this."

"Let's bring her sometime, when it's quieter." Grandma

loved Benton, even though she didn't remember him any more than she did Leah. Her eyes lit up at seeing him every time, and they sang old hymns together.

Looking up, Leah caught sight of the red, pink and white roses growing beside the staff cottage. "The roses look gorgeous. The garden staff has taken good care of them."

"Someone has, that's for sure. A little work's been done around the front of the house, too. Come see."

She hadn't been down the side street since January. How much had changed? Eagerly, she kept up with Benton's long-legged pace as he led her around the back and side of the house. Rounding the corner to the front, Leah gaped. "This isn't a little work, honey. It's a total overhaul."

The rickety fence had been replaced with a picket fence to match the one in the backyard, complete with a gate. Thick, green grass carpeted the front yard, bordered by new shrubs and flowers. The house looked ready for someone to move in, down to the adorable, bronze Arts and Crafts style mailbox, situated on a post that matched the porch columns. "It's beautiful."

"You like it?"

"I do. In fact, I want this exact mailbox someday. It's so cute." She patted the mailbox, then turned back, ambling back around the house so they could rejoin the others at the museum opening. "I half expected the museum to turn the house into offices or something, but I guess all of this yardwork means the museum council is putting the house on the market. If they can't use the space, they can benefit from the sale of the parcel."

"True, but my understanding is the money wasn't the main factor." They reached the backyard, and Benton stopped to lean against the porch railing. "Faith, Rowena, and the council thought a family should live here again."

"I agree." This house shouldn't sit empty. "I'm sure there will be a lot of interested buyers."

"It's already sold, actually."

Wow. "That's fast. Who bought it, do you know?"

"The new owner is a simple guy who's grown rather fond of the place."

His eyes twinkled, but there was something behind the spark. Something intense and smoldering. Vulnerable.

And then his words hit home.

"You bought the house?" Tears filled her eyes.

"I bought the house."

How? He'd used up all the money from selling this place on the church. "I don't understand. It must have cost a fortune."

"Not in its condition. The council knew I'd take good care of it, so they offered an excellent price." He closed the gap between them and took her hands. "While you were at endowment meetings, I pruned rosebushes and laid sod and replaced the fence. With a little help from friends, of course. The inside needs a lot of work to make it a home, but I'm hoping you'll help with that. I want to marry you, Leah. More than anything, I want to start a life with you, here in this house, unless you don't like it. But I remember what you said about the view and the rosebushes—"

"You want to marry me?"

"Maybe I should've said that first." He slipped down to one knee. Releasing her hands, he pulled a black box from the breast pocket of his blazer. Her hands went to her mouth as he pulled a sparkling solitaire from the black velvet. Beautiful as it was, it couldn't hold a candle to the light burning in his eyes. "Will you marry me, Leah?"

"Right this minute, I'd marry you." Her hands fell so he could slip the ring on the fourth finger of her left hand.

She pulled him to his feet, and he took her face in his strong, gentle hands. "Is that a yes?"

"Yes." She laughed. "Yes, I'll marry you."

They were both laughing when he pulled her into his arms and kissed her, but soon she couldn't laugh, much less breathe. She cherished his warmth, his closeness, the knowledge that soon he would be completely hers. Benton lifted his head, his eyes as dazed as she felt inside. Leah tugged his lapels so she could kiss him again.

"Eww," a high-pitched voice yelled.

"Nora, shh!"

Leah turned her head. A group clustered on Hughes House's back porch. Irene, Phil, Rowena, Marigold, the Lamberts, Clementine and her kids, Maude, and the Santos clan. Nora had a disgusted look on her face. "But Daddy, they were kissing."

"Bleah," her brother Logan agreed.

"It's about time," Rowena said, before blowing them a kiss.

Benton wrapped his arms around her and kissed her temple. "I didn't realize we had an audience. I'm sorry."

"Don't be." She laid her head against his chest. "We're part of a community, remember?"

"So when's the big day? Soon, I hope?" Kellan yelled. Kellan, as Leah recalled, had a short engagement himself.

"You'll all be the first to know," Leah yelled back, laughing, before lowering her voice for her fiancé. "What do you think?"

"I'll wait as long as you want, but I have to admit, my preference is soon."

"I want to be married by Christmas, so we can wake up Christmas morning here in this house," Leah decided. "From now on, every Christmas will be full of lights and joy and love."

"And gingerbread?"

"Absolutely, gingerbread."

A little spice and a whole lot of sweet. That was the sort of home they'd create together, for next Christmas, and all the Christmases to come.

* * * * *

If you enjoyed this story, look for the other books in this series:

A Future for His Twins
Seeking Sanctuary

Dear Reader,

Thank you for spending Christmas in Widow's Peak Creek with me! Christmas is one of my favorite times of the year. Along with celebrating the true meaning of the season, Jesus, I love the lights, the decorations, the music, and yes, gingerbread houses! Unfortunately, I'm not gifted at decorating them, but I never pass up an opportunity to view the amazing gingerbread creations others come up with: churches, castles, barns and more. Gingerbread houses make me feel like a kid again!

I hope you enjoyed Benton and Leah's gingerbread Christmas story. Both had to lean on God for strength as they navigated rough patches. We all have difficult seasons and circumstances. Learning to fully trust God and live into the joy of His love is not always easy—but it's the most wonderful, excellent way to live!

If you'd guessed that Clementine will soon get a happily-ever-after of her own, you're right! She's next to meet her match in Widow's Peak Creek—with a little help from matchmakers both old and young.

Until then, please know how grateful I am to you, readers, for your support of Christian fiction. I'd love to connect on my website, www.SusanneDietze.com, on Facebook at SusanneDietzeBooks, or Instagram and Twitter as SusanneDietze. Merry Christmas!

Blessings,
Susanne

"Are you okay?" Stone asked, tightening his hold around her waist and gripping one of her hands.

"I— Yes." She didn't have time to explain to Stone why this had nothing to do with her sore ankle, nor why avalanches were her worst nightmare and that was the real reason why she'd suddenly swayed in his arms.

Not when there was work to be done. There were people in Holden Springs who needed help, and she knew she should be there.

Tugger whined and pressed against her leg as he'd been taught to do as a therapy dog. He could tell her heart rate had increased and her pulse was pounding in her ears, even if she didn't show it in her expression, although there was probably that, too. The dog was responding to cues most humans couldn't see, and Felicity reached out and absently ran a hand between Tugger's ears to steady her insides.

"Have they set up a temporary disaster shelter yet?" she asked.

"Yes. At Holden High School," her sister said. "They're using the cafeteria and the gym, I think. I'd go myself except I have clients in the middle of service dog training back at the center. Do you mind taking Tugger and heading out there?"

Felicity did mind. More than anyone would ever know, because she never talked about it, not even to her siblings. But now was not the time to give in to those feelings. She could cry into her pillow later when she was alone and the people of Holden Springs were safe.

"I'll take Tugger." She nodded. "And Dandy, too," she said, referring to a young black Labrador retriever who was part of the therapy dog program.

"I can tag along, if there's anything I can do to assist," Stone said. "That way you'll have an extra person for the dogs."

Felicity was going to decline, but Ruby spoke up first. "Thank you, Stone. They need all the help they can get. From what I hear, there are a lot of families who were suddenly evacuated from their homes."

"It's settled, then," Stone said. "I'm going with you."

Felicity didn't feel settled. The last thing she needed was Stone alongside her. It would distract her from her real work.

She sighed deeply.

A bruised ankle.

Stone's unnerving presence.

And now an avalanche.

Could things get any worse?

Don't miss
Their Unbreakable Bond *by Deb Kastner,*
available January 2022 wherever
Love Inspired books and ebooks are sold.

LoveInspired.com

LIEXP1221